Peter Cave left school at 16 and became a printing apprentice on the *Herald Express*, Torquay. He later became a reporter on a magazine, and then magazine editor before leaving for the South of France where he sang folk songs in cafes for centimes.

Sometime later Peter Cave began to write short stories, and formed an agency called Space Features with Christopher Priest, who was to become one of Britain's leading science-fiction writers. Peter Cave ended up as freelance editor of six magazines and took up writing seri[illegible] His bestseller *Chopper* was published in 1[illegible]

Peter Cave

The New Avengers 1: House of Cards

Futura Publications Limited
A Futura Book

A Futura Book

First published in Great Britain in 1976 by
Futura Publications Limited

ISBN 0 8600 7472 2

Printed in Great Britain by
Hazell Watson & Viney Ltd
Aylesbury, Bucks

Futura Publications Limited
110 Warner Road, Camberwell
London SE5

PROLOGUE

John F. Kennedy was dead. Lee Harvey Oswald was dead. Jack Ruby sat, as silent as a zombie in his prison cell, revealing nothing. Soon he too would be dead and with him would die the answer to the mystery which had baffled the world.

Nikolai Perov felt a warm glow of satisfaction deep inside, despite the fact that he stood in the Siberian tundra, with the temperature well below zero. It was time to move. While the West reeled under the shock, he would initiate his master-plan to hot up the cold war once and for all.

He turned, facing the small village he had had specially built in the middle of the icy wasteland. It looked incongruous – not only because no human being could normally survive there. The buildings were strange. Alien. Even the name of the village was wrong. The wooden signpost on its outskirts was in an unnatural language, even the characters oddly different.

Little Warehampton, the sign read. A strange name indeed for a place in Siberia.

Perov smiled to himself, striding quickly through the snow towards one of the buildings. A pub . . . an English pub.

Perov strolled into the public bar of the Queen's Arms, grinning jovially at the regulars who clustered around the welcoming warmth of the roaring log fire.

An unwanted sight wiped the smile from his face. Perov walked quickly across the bar to a table, where two men sat over their drinks. He reached down, snatching a glass of vodka from the hand of the man nearest to him.

'What is this?' he demanded angrily. 'You had your orders. There was to be no vodka. Here, you drink beer, or Scotch whisky.'

He dashed the glass to the floor, his face dark with rage. The man stood up, nervously, his face apologetic. 'Forgive me, comrade,' he whined. 'It is just that I hate the taste of that English beer . . . foul stuff that it is. A little glass of comfort, comrade . . . a taste of home, to keep out the cold.'

Perov's hand snaked out, lashing the man across the face. 'Fool,' he spat explosively. 'Not content with one foolish mistake, you dare to make another.'

'Another?' the quivering man asked, not aware of the sin he had committed.

'You called me "comrade",' Perov hissed. 'That mistake can not be forgiven.'

He raised his hand, snapping his fingers. Two other men stood, crossing the bar to him to carry out his bidding. Perov jerked his head impassively to the cowering man before him. 'Take him outside,' he snapped. 'You know what to do.'

The two men seized their screaming, struggling companion and dragged him out of the pub. A few moments later, came the sound of a single gunshot. The two men returned.

Perov nodded to himself. Nothing had happened that he had not accounted for. There were bound to be a proportion of failures, rejects. He seated himself at the table with the second man, who sat sipping at a pint of bitter quite contentedly. Perov smiled at him warmly.

'Ah, Ivan Kerineska, you will not let me down, will you?'

His companion smiled back, saying nothing.

Perov clapped him on the back, laughing out loud. 'No, you will not let me down.' he repeated. 'You will do exactly what I want you to do. You will become David Milner. You will become respected, and prosperous. In time, you will become a very close friend of John Steed.'

CHAPTER 1

'Well, how do I look?'

Purdey swept into the room with a grand gesture, twirling a multi-coloured kaftan about her lithe body and inviting Steed's inspection.

He glanced up, grinning as his keen eyes took in the garish clothes and beads, the wild, frizzy Afro wig and the bizarre eye make-up. 'Weird,' he muttered softly.

Purdey framed her plum-coloured lips into a soft pout. 'The word is freaky,' she corrected gently. 'And pop fans are *supposed* to look freaky.' She broke off to cross the room and take a fresh look at herself in the mirror. The sight caused her to dissolve into helpless laughter. 'Just wait until you see Mike,' she warned, turning back to Steed.

Steed allowed himself another wry smile. 'I can't wait,' he purred sarcastically.

'You don't have to.' Mike Gambit made his own entrance, with considerably less flair than Purdey. He lurked, sheepishly, in the doorway, plainly embarrassed by his own outlandish appearance.

Steed gazed at him in disbelief. His colleague was virtually unrecognizable. 'Purdey, you've excelled yourself,' he whispered in awe. 'He looks absolutely . . . what was that word again?'

'Freaky,' Purdey put in. 'In fact, though I say it myself, superfreaky.'

'I must say I don't feel freaky,' complained Gambit. 'Stupid is more the word I would have chosen. Would someone please tell me what all this is about?'

He walked precariously across the room towards his two colleagues, acutely conscious of the unbalancing effect of the eight-inch heels on the silver boots which he wore. Reaching the sofa, he lowered his silver laméd frame gingerly down into it with a metallic rustle. Sitting back, Gambit regarded Steed and Purdey moodily from underneath much-mascaraed and glitter-dusted eyelids.

'You're beautiful,' Purdey joked, trying to lift his spirits.

Gambit grunted angrily, turning his attention to Steed. 'Steed, will you please tell me why I am dressed up in this ridiculous garb?'

The smile on Steed's face faded. The joking was over. It was time to talk business. 'Vasil,' he murmured. 'Anton Vasil.'

Gambit whistled softly under his breath. 'Professor Vasil?'

Steed nodded. 'The professor himself. Probably the world's leading expert on forced-reactor nuclear breeding. Professor Vasil is at this minute taking a little trip.'

'Where to?'

'Heathrow,' Steed answered simply. 'Our much-respected professor is paying us a visit. Somewhat of a permanent visit, we very much hope.'

Mike Gambit's mouth dropped open in astonishment. 'He's planning to defect? With all that knowledge inside his head? They'll never let him get away with it.'

Steed nodded grimly. 'Exactly. Vasil is going to need a little help. Our help. He's flying in this afternoon on a scheduled flight from Prague. My guess is that there'll be a reception committee waiting for him.'

'Should be some reception,' Purdey put in. 'Warm, to say the least.'

'Extremely,' Steed agreed. 'The word is that they will

gun him down on sight. They can't risk Vasil giving any of his research secrets to the West. The stakes are too high. With what Vasil knows, and our own research at Windscale, we could have a virtual nuclear monopoly within three years.'

'That still doesn't explain why I'm dressed up like a Martian,' Gambit said. 'Would someone kindly care to explain?'

'Your day of glory is at hand,' Purdey murmured, mysteriously. 'For the next few precious hours, you can savour the sweet taste of fame. Today, you are no longer Mike Gambit.'

'Oh.' Gambit digested this information slowly. 'So who am I?'

'Pretty Boy Power,' Steed said, his voice betraying the faintest trace of a chuckle beneath the words. 'Pop star extraordinaire, showman and idol, revered by countless millions of screaming teenyboppers the world over.' He turned to Purdey. 'Did you manage to line up the million screaming teenyboppers?'

Purdey nodded briefly. 'A hundred and twenty. It was the best I could do in the time. Culled, I might add, from the best drama schools in London, and their lungs rehearsed to bursting point.'

'Fine.' Steed rose, reaching out for his bowler and patting it into place upon his head with his customary flourish. 'Shall we go, then?'

Gambit was still muttering underneath his breath as they walked through the door. 'I still wish someone would tell me exactly what's going on.'

Purdey slipped her arm around his shoulders, patting him reassuringly. 'I promise I'll explain everything in the car,' she told him.

The ill-assorted trio sat in a small private waiting room attached to the airport's VIP lounge. Gambit fidgeted with the gleaming electric guitar Purdey had thrust into his grasp. 'You realize I can't play a note?'

Steed glanced at him questioningly, then a slow smile of understanding dawned on his face. 'Of course, I forgot to explain about that,' he murmured. 'A small oversight on my part.' He prodded a finger down at the instrument. 'You don't have to play this little gadget,' he explained. 'It plays its own very deadly little tune.'

Gambit examined the guitar more closely, suddenly understanding. Concealed under the dazzling array of coloured plastic and gleaming chrome knobs was a high-powered rifle.

'The trigger is that tremolo arm,' Steed added, helpfully. 'It'll fire twelve rounds – quietly. The silencer is built in.' He glanced down at his watch. 'Vasil's plane is due in any moment now. You both understand what you have have to do?'

Gambit and Purdey nodded silently.

'Good,' Steed said, rising to his feet. 'I suggest you go and round up Mike's little fan club, Purdey.'

'Right.' She set off in search of her teenage army.

Steed turned to Gambit. 'Let's go,' he said quietly. 'Stay well behind me and keep your eyes open.'

The two men strode purposefully along the corridor leading to the VIP arrival lounge. In the background, the heavy drone of the approaching Ilyushin heralded the imminent arrival of their important guest.

Steed took up a position near a bank of wall telephones, seemingly casual although his trained eyes were working overtime. In a matter of seconds, Steed had given every man in the place a thorough going-over. He did not care much for what he saw. Professor Vasil was certainly getting a high-powered reception committee

. . . five strong, and headed by no less a personage than Nikolai Perov himself.

Steed's lips compressed into a thin line as he hissed the name to himself. Perov! Perhaps his oldest, and most elusive enemy. For over twenty years now, Nikolai Perov had been the central figure in an espionage network which covered most of Free Europe. Yet no-one had ever been able to nail him. Assassinations, kidnappings, double-agents and double-deals. Perov was the master of them all, and always one step ahead of the opposition. Steed allowed himself a grim smile at the prospect of a new and direct encounter with his old adversary. Their paths had crossed often before, but never for such high stakes.

With a cool detachment, Steed summed up the rest of the opposition and his chances. Of Perov's colleagues, Steed recognized only two: Boris Grnaud and the man known as Kristos. The other men were fairly standard 'heavies' – faceless men trained to appear, kill, then melt into obscurity until their deadly talents were needed again. Without Steed's intervention, Professor Vasil stood no chance at all.

The plane had landed and the passengers were on their way across the tarmac in the courtesy coach. Perov and his men started to make their way towards the arrival gates, moving separately, yet with the uncanny gestalt of worker ants, or bees. Steed watched two of the heavies reach deep into their topcoat pockets, noting the telltale bulges as their fists closed around the butts and triggers of pistols.

Their timing was superb. They reached the arrival gates at the very instant Vasil stepped through them, falling neatly into place either side of him as Perov appeared out of nowhere to confront the professor face to face.

Steed saw the fear on Vasil's face, quickly followed by a look of utter resignation. Flanked by his unwanted escort, the professor began to trudge wearily towards the exit.

Steed muttered to himself under his breath. 'Come on Purdey, where are you?' His gaze darted over to where Gambit had emerged from his hiding place in the rest-room, placing himself in direct line between the approaching group and the main exit.

A chorus of blood-curdling screams ripped into Steed's concentration. From the opposite side of the lounge Purdey and her screamy-bopper army threw themselves whole-heartedly into creating their planned diversion. Mike Gambit paled under the heavy make-up on his face as the teenage horde rushed towards him.

Perov and his cronies were also thrown by the sudden noise. They looked round nervously as the wave of fake fans swept towards them, seemingly oblivious of anyone or anything between them and their idol.

Suddenly the entire lounge was in a state of pandemonium. Casual onlookers were swept aside, knocked to the floor and trampled on as the screaming girls closed in for the kill. Purdey led the way, screaming at the top of her voice. 'Pretty Boy, Pretty Boy. Welcome to England.'

Steed moved quickly now, racing across the intervening space towards Perov and his confused comrades. As the mob of girls surged around them, knocking Boris and Kristos flying, Steed moved into position behind the two men pressed against Professor Vasil. With a deceptively innocent gesture, Steed raised his fingers to the brim of his bowler. The heavy steel lining cracked down on top of Boris's head, stunning him immediately. As the man crumpled to the ground, and his companion began to turn in alarm, Steed's knee jabbed up into his groin, viciously. The man doubled up in pain, his gun-hand jerking free from his pocket in involuntary reaction. Steed swung the brim of his metal-clad bowler against the man's throat. Clawing and choking, he fought for breath, while the death-rattle sounded in his throat. He too sank to the floor. Steed stepped forward smartly, sliding his hand neatly under Professor Vasil's elbow. 'Shall we go, Professor. Things seem a trifle hectic here.'

Vasil, totally confused, allowed himself to be led away at a loping run. Perov, swept aside in the first onslaught of Purdey's teenage army, recovered himself quickly. His hand darted into the inside of his jacket, emerging with a small but deadly automatic. The gun came up quickly, lined up directly with Vasil's departing back.

Purdey was right behind him. She cannoned into his back, her bunched knuckles slamming into his kidneys. With a grunt of pain, Perov stiffened, releasing a single, harmless shot into the air.

Steed and Professor Vasil were almost at the exit doors. Gambit, swinging the deadly guitar into firing position, covered them. Only one other heavy managed to escape from the mêlée for long enough to draw a gun and take aim. He never had the chance to squeeze the trigger. The guitar in Gambit's hands jumped slightly, a faint hum from the strings covering the slight plopping sound of the silenced barrel. The would-be gunman threw up his arms and fell backwards under the impact of the high-velocity slug chewing into the centre of his chest.

Purdey's screaming pop fans were still in full voice, joined now by the yells and cries of panicking by-standers. There was a general rush for the exits. Perov and his cronies took the full brunt of the onslaught, disappearing beneath a wave of trampling feet as Steed and Vasil made it to the exit and raced across the taxi area towards their waiting car.

'Keep your head down,' Steed barked to Vasil as they bundled into the black Rover.

It was a warning with good reason. Steed had counted on Perov placing other men outside the terminal buildings. He was right. Half a dozen bullets ripped into the bodywork and rear window of the car as it screamed away leaving black rubber-scorches on the grey cemented surface of the car park.

The car's driver, protected by a bullet-proof glass plate between himself and the rear passenger section, drove quickly, but without panic. Steed smiled disarmingly at the cowering professor. 'Good chap, Roland,' he muttered, jerking a thumb casually towards the front driving seat. 'Grows roses, y'know.'

Two more rifle bullets found their way through the shattered rear window. Vasil cringed even more, pressing himself to the car's floor with a little whimper of fear.

'Get any time for gardening yourself, Professor?' Steed asked, conversationally.

Vasil croaked. 'I just try to stay alive,' he managed to blurt out.

Steed chuckled, straightening up in the seat now that he knew they were out of accurate range. Reaching down, he slipped his arm under Vasil's armpit and urged him to his feet. 'Not your problem any longer, old chap,' he muttered. Then, glancing back through the bullet-riddled rear window: 'More a problem for for old Perov, I should say. Now that he's bungled this one.'

In the airport terminal, Pretty Boy Power's career came to an end as quickly as it had begun. Purdey's recruited teenyboppers dispersed into the crowd and went their separate ways. Gambit and Purdey sneaked out the back way to their own waiting car. Gradually, the panic subsided, leaving in its wake two dead men, several confused assassins and an ashen-faced, trembling Perov.

He had good cause to tremble. If anyone knew the price of failure it was Perov. He had shipped enough bodies across Europe in wooden crates to know only too well.

In the fleeing Rover, Steed produced a bottle of Remy Martin and two crystal goblets. 'Lovely day,' he purred, grinning again. 'Such a lovely day, I think we ought to take a little spin in the country.'

Vasil, his fingers still shaking, accepted the proffered drink, reflecting miserably upon the insanity of the English.

CHAPTER 2

Nikolai Perov carried the world upon his shoulders. Its prodigious weight bowed his back, slumped his head forwards. He sat, a lone and frightened man, in his private office deep in the inner recesses of the embassy. Immobile, he gazed blankly down into the smooth and polished teak surface of his desk.

An intercom buzzed softly, fell silent for a few seconds and then sounded again, more insistently. Perov's hand moved towards it slowly, almost unwillingly. Wearily, he flipped the switch. 'Ya?'

Olga Perinkov's clipped, businesslike voice came over the speaker. 'You have not made your report, comrade Perov. I must cable the Commissariat within the hour.'

Perov's voice was hoarse, distant. 'Come in to my office, Olga.' He snapped off the intercom switch, sat back in his chair and tried to pull himself up into a more imposing posture.

The door opened silently. Olga Perinkov stepped in, her trim legs carrying her neatly and efficiently to Perov's side. She held a notebook and pen in her hands and looked the epitome of the efficient private secretary. Only the slightest trace of a Slavic accent in her voice, and the secret she shared with Perov could have betrayed her as anything more than that. In reality, she occupied a highly important post in her country's espionage network. To all intents and purposes, she was Perov's direct second-in-command.

'The operation went as planned?' she asked, hardly expecting anything more than a curt affirmation.

Perov swung round in his swivel chair to face her directly. He had trouble looking directly into her eyes. 'We failed, Olga,' he muttered, wearily. 'Or rather, I failed.'

Only the faintest trace of emotion showed, fractionally, upon Olga's beautiful face. She raised one neatly-groomed eyebrow. 'Failed, comrade?'

Perov nodded. 'Vasil escaped . . . was rescued.' There was a catch in his voice.

'Rescued . . . how?' Olga demanded.

It was the final ignominy. Perov buried his face in his hands. 'I was tricked, Olga . . . tricked by a bunch of screaming schoolgirls. The shame of it . . . it is too much to bear.'

A fleeting look of scorn passed over Olga's face. Then, pulling herself together, she reassumed her bland, expressionless facade. 'You realize what this means, comrade?' she murmured gently. A note of apology crept into her voice. 'I will have to make a full report. I can leave nothing out.'

'Yes, Olga, yes.' Perov nodded his head violently. 'I know you must do your job . . . as I should have done mine.'

'Perhaps they will be sympathetic,' Olga suggested. 'They must remember your wonderful work on the House of Cards operation. That must count for something. Even this – a failure of such monumental proportions.'

'Perhaps,' Perov muttered, without any real hope or expectancy in his voice. 'But there is only one Professor Vasil, and my past work is insignificant against his loss.'

There was no argument to offer against that statement. Olga merely nodded her blonde head reflectively, and turned neatly on her heel. 'I must go and make my report,' she said curtly, as she left the room, closing the door quietly behind her.

Faintly, from the outer office, Perov heard the clicks of the teletype machine as Olga began transmitting her coded message home. He sighed heavily, a man suddenly gifted with second sight and the sure knowledge of his own fate. Perov knew exactly what message would come back on that same machine. His immediate return . . . a private plane sent to pick him up . . . his own men escorting him to it under armed guard and close arrest. Then, once home . . . an accident, a sudden disappearance . . . perhaps vicious repercussions against his family. The price of failure was high.

. . . And yet . . . maybe there *could* be a little hope. Olga had mentioned the House of Cards. She was right, it had been a daring, and highly successful operation. It might make a difference . . . perhaps only to commute his death sentence to a form of life in one of the camps, or in the mines.

The House of Cards . . . A fleeting, thin smile crossed his lips as he remembered. Thirteen years ago – when he, Nikolai Perov had been at the height of his career. A plan of such novelty and cunning that he had been raised two places in the inner hierarchy almost overnight for his conception and execution of it.

Perov stood up, crossing his office towards his private wall-safe. He alone knew the combination. Even Olga, despite her own high position, did not share the secret of the House of Cards with Perov and a small handful of top ministers in the government itself.

Dialling the seven numbers, Perov swung the safe open, drawing out the thick red folder inside. Returning to his desk, he reached underneath it and flipped the concealed switch which operated the security locks on all doors to his inner office. Only then did he dare break the wax seal of the folder and begin to pull out its top-secret contents.

In the outer office, Olga Perinkov straightened up from the teletype machine and stared at the printed reply she had ripped off. Her agile mind decoded the message quickly. A gloating smile of satisfaction spread across her face, turning her beauty into a more sinister mask for a few moments.

Her orders were exactly what she had expected them to be. She would take over immediately. The top job was hers now, along with all the secrets and the power that it entailed. Now she alone would have the combination to that wall-safe, and the power of life and death over dozens of Britain's top agents.

She moved, with a new briskness, to the intercom, and flipped the switch. 'Comrade Perov. Your are recalled immediately. Your flight will arrive at the private airfield at 09.32 hours precisely. You are to turn over all current and relevant documents to me at once.' She paused before her next words. They came out with something less than the absolute ring of truth. 'You have my sympathy, comrade.'

Perov's hoarse voice filtered through the speaker. 'I understand, Olga. It is as I expected. You will do well. You are a fine woman.' He broke off. Through the intercom, Olga heard the sound of a sliding desk drawer and the faint clink of glass upon the desk's hard surface.

Intuitively, she ran to the sealed door, pounding upon it. 'Perov, I must demand that you release these security locks at once. You can only make matters worse for yourself.'

Perov's faint, ironic chuckle sounded chillingly over the intercom. 'Worse, Olga? What can be worse for me now? Alas, much as I hate to start your new career on a sour note, I fear I must prevent you from fulfilling your first task, Olga. You too must learn to cope with failure. That alone, I could perhaps bear. I could face my failure, but I cannot face my shame, and the laughter.'

The intercom went dead. With a faint click, the security locks snapped back. Olga pushed the doors open quickly, rushing into the inner office.

She saw what she had expected to see. Perov lay slumped, face-down, over his desk. A few inches from his nerveless fingers lay an empty hypodermic syringe, a few drops of liquid still bubbling from its tip.

Olga's face knitted up. Grimly, she reviewed her position. The Commissariat would not be pleased to have lost Comrade Perov so easily. They would censure her, that was certain.

Yet . . . little was really lost. Perov's premature death was only a triviality. He would just fail to answer some questions, that was all. Certain skilled persuaders would lose a little sadistic pleasure.

Olga rallied herself. She should get off with little more than a mild rebuke. She was not really to blame. Perov's devious cunning was legendary. It was no real surprise that he had outsmarted them all, even in the final analysis.

Turning away from the corpse, Olga's eyes strayed to the concealed wall-safe. It was closed. She strode, briskly across to it and dialled up the newly-acquired combination. Glancing inside, she ran her eyes over the red folder and smiled briefly.

For a moment, her fingers itched to pull out the file and learn its secrets. Then, reluctantly, they withdrew. There was more immediate work to be done. Perov's funeral to arrange, for a start. Olga slammed the safe shut and spun the dial, scrambling the combination once again. Tempting though it was, the House of Cards mystery could wait a little longer to reveal its intricacies.

The cremation service was a simple one, attended only by Olga, a handful of officials from the Embassy, and two or three of Perov's few personal friends. Steed hovered in the background, at the rear of the crematorium. He watched, with a certain sadness, as the plain coffin bearing the remains of Nikolai Perov moved smoothly along the conveyor belt, through the plush red velvet curtain to the flames beyond. There was a dull roar as the gas-fired oven was boosted to full heat, gradually subsiding into a final, complete, silence.

Steed's regrets were genuine enough. There was a certain bond between enemies, just as there was between close friends. Despite their chosen positions on opposite sides of the political fence, Steed had always felt a grudging respect for his late adversary. Perov had been a clever, and cunning man. It warmed Steed's heart slightly to realize that even at the end, Perov had still retained at least one little trick up his sleeve.

He turned away towards the exit. His eyes met Olga's. She stood, draped in black. Somehow, she made even mourning clothes seem the height of fashionable elegance.

Steed stepped up to her, stopped and extended his hand. Olga presented her fingers, palm-down. Clutching them gently, Steed stooped slightly to plant a light kiss on the back of her hand. 'My beautiful Olga,' he whispered quietly. 'My most favourite, and most ravishing spy.'

Olga clucked her tongue reprovingly. 'Steed,' she

chided. 'Why on earth must you use that ugly . . . and so inaccurate . . . word? I am a Cultural Attaché. You know that.'

Steed smiled slyly. 'Ah yes, of course. We live in the age of euphemisms.'

A flash of anger betrayed itself on Olga's normally emotionless face. 'You must always make these insulting jokes.'

Steed shrugged apologetically. 'Make jokes . . . not war?' he suggested, sauvely.

Olga raised an eyebrow. 'I thought it was "make love . . . not war".'

Steed raised his eyes, rolling them suggestively. 'Ah, what a delicious thought,' he murmured, distantly. 'Who knows? Perhaps, one day, you might have to seduce me in the name of the cause. I am sure, my dearest Olga, that you would put Mata Hari to shame.'

Olga snatched her hand away abruptly. Her eyes narrowed. 'You came to see poor Perov off. It is appreciated,' she snapped. 'Now, perhaps you will excuse me? I have much work to do.'

Steed nodded sympathetically. 'Of course. It's a busy life being a . . . Cultural Attaché,' he murmured, the accent on the last two words unmistakable. 'All work and no play, I fear. Not even time perhaps to play a game . . . of cards?'

Steed was staring intently into her eyes. Despite her immense self-control, Olga was unable to conceal the flash of reaction which momentarily crossed them, betraying her. She spun on the balls of her feet, walking away at a faster pace than the reverence of the occasion would normally demand.

Steed followed her out of the small crematorium, closing the door behind him.

Inside, behind the velvet curtains, a cadaverous individual named Cartney peered moodily into the dwindling flames licking around the crumbled ashes of the coffin. He turned to the man standing beside him. 'Such a splendid way to go, don't you agree?'

Nikolai Perov, very much alive, chuckled under his breath. 'Indeed,' he agreed. 'May I rest in peace.' He beamed upon Cartney. 'Clever little device, that drug of yours,' he complimented the man. 'Very clever indeed. To suspend heartbeat and respiration so completely, for twenty-four hours. A small taste of death – with a long and happy life still to come at the end of it.'

'Happy?' Cartney queried, doubtfully.

Perov smiled. 'Ah yes, my dear Cartney. There is great happiness to be found in revenge.' He delved into his pocket, fishing out a small bundle of playing cards. He shuffled them in his hand. 'Pick a card, Cartney . . . any card you choose.'

Cartney selected a card at random, pulling it from the concealment of Perov's grasp. He stared at it in surprise as he realized that it was only the top of the King of Hearts. Not understanding, he turned it over slowly. Printed on the reverse side was a single name.

Steed.

Perov, glancing down at it, beamed with satisfaction. 'Ah, an excellent choice, Cartney. I couldn't have chosen better myself.' He rubbed his hands together. 'Yes indeed, a very fitting choice.'

CHAPTER 3

'Any mail?'

David Milner glanced up briefly from the breakfast table as his wife returned from her trip to pick up the morning milk.

'Only this.' Carelessly, Suzy Milner tossed a small buff envelope on to the table beside the toast rack.

With equal casualness, Milner picked it up, smearing a little marmalade across its flap as he did so. Neatly, he flipped the envelope open and fished inside for the small piece of pasteboard which it contained.

Suzy had already turned back to the grill, to supervise her husband's bacon. She heard only a stifled scream, and the sound of David Milner crashing from his chair to the breakfast room floor.

'David, what is it?' she cried in panic, running to his side and bending over him.

Milner's hands were pressed against the side of his head, as though he were suffering some terrible physical or mental terror. His eyes rolled convulsively, exposing the whites, while his whole body twitched with explosive spasms. A horrible, curdling scream was ripped from his throat to pass across pale lips. Then the fit, or whatever it was, passed as quickly as it had taken him.

Suzy stood, trembling, as her husband slowly crawled to his feet. 'My God, David, what was it? Epilepsy? You never told me . . .'

David Milner fought to regain himself, slowly shaking his hand. Between gasps for breath, he hastened to reassure her. 'It's all right now, Suzy. It's all right. I fought it, Suzy . . . the conditioning. It's gone now, gone.'

He lowered himself gently back into his chair, slumping across the table. The half-playing card was just out of his immediate range of vision. Sucking in a deep breath, Milner forced himself to look at it again, and a fresh, but shallow tremor shook his body once more, subsiding quickly

He nodded wearily, as if in final affirmation. 'Yes, it's passed now.' He pushed himself to his feet, a sense of urgency etched into his face. 'You must leave at once, Suzy . . . this morning. Go to the cottage . . . our safe place. I'll join you there as soon as I can.'

Suzy's eyes rose to meet those of her husband. They bore a tinge of fear. 'It's happened, then?'

Milner nodded. 'We always knew it might . . . one day. I had hoped . . . that it was all dead and buried . . . forgotten.' He reached out to grasp his wife by both hands. Pulling her to him briefly, he thrust her away, gently. 'There's no time to lose. You must go at once. Stop for no-one.'

Suzy Milner regarded her husband for a few seconds, finally nodding blankly. She knew what to do, even though she did not fully understand why. She detached herself from him. 'I'll go and pack a few things,' she muttered, backing away.

Milner waited until the sound of his wife's Mini faded into the distance before reaching for the telephone. Urgently, he flipped through his address book before dialling Steed's ex-directory number out at the stud farm.

Outside the house, a heavily-disguised Perov sat beside Cartney in the front seat of a dark blue Citroen. Both men watched Suzy Milner drive away from the house at top speed.

'He's sent his wife packing,' Cartney observed. 'Hardly the right reaction, would you say?'

Perov sighed. 'No more than I expected, really. Milner was always the weakest link in the chain . . . the one I was never quite sure of. He had a strong mind, did Milner. I often suspected that he resisted the conditioning.'

As he spoke, he pulled a gun from his pocket and began to screw a silencer on to the end of the barrel. 'Still, it is of little matter,' he murmured, climbing out of the car.

Cartney sat, impassive, as Petrov strode up David Milner's front drive. Producing a pass-key, Perov let himself quietly in the front door.

'Damn you Steed, answer,' Milner hissed under his breath as the insistent purring of the telephone repeated itself over and over. Stretching the receiver as far as he could away from the cradle, he crossed to the French windows and looked out into the ground towards the paddock. He slipped down the catch and threw the glass door open.

He moved back towards the telephone table, slipping out a small drawer underneath it and extracting a small, snub-nose Mauser. Flipping off the safety-catch, he held it ready in his free hand.

There was the faintest metallic creak from the lounge door. Milner's eyes flashed over there immediately as the old-fashioned wrought-iron handle began to turn, very very gently. He brought the Mauser up, squeezing six shots into the woodwork of the door, about chest-high on a normal man. Then, dropping the telephone to the floor, he broke into a run, fleeing through the open French windows towards the stables.

On the other side of the lounge door, Perov looked up from his kneeling position at the six jagged holes where the bullets had splintered their way through the wood. He smiled to himself. He was too old a dog to put himself in the firing line. Standing, he pushed down the handle, kicked at the door and threw himself sideways behind the portal.

The door flew open into an empty room. Satisfied that Milner had fled, Perov stepped in, his keen eyes running around every square inch of the lounge. Seeing the dangling phone, he stepped across and lifted it to his ear – just as Steed answered it at the other end.

'Steed. Who is it?'

Perov smiled to himself. Milner had reacted exactly as planned. He placed his lips close to the mouthpiece. 'I'm terribly sorry you've been troubled, Mr Steed.' He slipped the telephone back into its cradle cutting the call off.

Hurrying across to the open French windows, Perov peered out, just in time to see David Milner gallop out of the stables on a black mare. Grinning, Perov brought his gun up slowly, with the assurance of a trained marksman. He squinted along the sights, taking careful aim. His finger caressed the trigger lightly, lovingly. Killing was such a deliciously subtle pleasure – open to few. They had no idea of just how much they were missing.

With an abrupt movement, he lowered the gun, slipping it back into his pocket. Now was not the right moment for that special pleasure. It would not quite suit his plans. Nikolai Perov was very particular about his plans. Precision was one of the faculties he had been most noted for . . . before his unfortunate death. Chuckling, Perov returned to Cartney in the car. 'Think you can beat a horse to Steed's place?' he enquired casually.

The Citroen squealed away from the kerb, heading out into the open countryside.

Back at the Embassy, Olga Perinkov crossed the office to her late lamented colleague's wall-safe for the second time in her life. She opened it and pulled out the House of Cards file, carrying it to the desk and sitting down to digest its contents. She was feeling very pleased with herself.

The contents of the folder spilled out on the surface of the desk. Olga picked up the deck of half-cards, smiling at the cunning and secrecy of the plan.

There was something wrong! Olga's sensitive fingers flashed a message of panic to her equally sensitive brain. The pack was too flimsy, too thin.

In desperation, she shuffled the half-cards out in front of her, spreading them across the desk. The fault was apparent in seconds. The entire suit of Hearts was missing!

With this realization came the sudden, terrible knowledge that Perov had tricked her yet again. Her shoulders slumped. Cold fear rippled through her body.

'Oh my God,' she half-sobbed, half-whispered to herself. 'The cunning bastard activated the House of Cards before his death.'

CHAPTER 4

Steed replaced the telephone receiver slowly. His normally placid face was creased with worry. There had been something about that voice . . .

Preoccupied, he returned to the billiards room to take up his solo game where he had left off. Gambit, passing the door on his way through to the gym for a workout, couldn't fail to notice Steed's unaccustomed frown.

'Something wrong?'

Steed shook his head slowly. 'Maybe . . . I don't really know. It could have been a wrong number, I suppose.'

Gambit shrugged. 'Not with you, Steed.'

Steed explained. 'The telephone rang . . . for quite a long time. I didn't hurry to answer it because I was playing out a sixty-eight break. When I did . . . the caller hung up. The line went dead.'

'Dead?' Gambit repeated.

For a split second, the word jumped in Steed's subconscious, as if a cell, or nerve, in his brain had received a tiny electrical charge. Then it was gone, without ever quite making the conscious connection. Steed forced the trivial worry from his mind. His face cleared. 'It's nothing. I must be getting jittery in my declining years,' he joked.

'Yeah,' Gambit grinned back. 'Look, Steed, I hope you don't mind me coming out to use the gym.'

Steed shook his head, 'Of course not. Got something special in mind?'

Gambit nodded. 'Strangest thing,' he murmured.

'Got a telephone call from Bill Spencer this morning. Haven't seen him in nearly five years.'

'Spence?' Steed asked, equally surprised. 'What did he want?'

Gambit laughed. 'Believe it or not, he said he was worried I might be getting a little rusty. Suggested he came out and put me through my paces.'

Steed clicked his tongue behind his teeth. 'Should be worth watching,' he said. 'I might well come along and watch, when I've finished this game.'

'No contest,' Gambit said with assurance. 'Spence might have taught me everything he knew, but I have a feeling that the pupil has well outstripped the master by now.'

Steed wasn't so sure. Bill Spencer had been the finest instructor in unarmed combat and the Oriental fighting arts in the country. He might well still be. Steed chuckled at Gambit's self-confidence. 'We'll see,' he said guardedly.

He turned back to the billiard table as Gambit gave him a quick thumbs-up sign and continued on his way to the gymnasium. Steed picked up his cue and bent over the table once more, taking in the position of the balls. There was a short, easy push shot on a red into the corner pocket. Played correctly, it should bring back the cue-ball into a good line-up for the pink. Steed, took it . . . and muffed it. The red went down, but the cue-ball spun off the cushion too hard, burying itself between another red and the yellow. He had snookered himself.

Steed straightened up to consider his next shot, realizing that his concentration was no longer fully on the game. A vague uneasiness still lurked at the back of his mind, putting him off his stroke.

A faint sound immediately behind him suddenly

snapped those powers of concentration into top gear again. A footstep. A very quiet, and furtive footstep.

Steed's incredibly agile mind worked through all the possibilities in milliseconds. Gambit, returning to speak to him again? No. Steed dismissed that possibility at once. Mike Gambit had been wearing soft shoes. The sound he had heard was of a leather heel on the parquet flooring of the games room.

Then the intruder was not a friend. Friends did not sneak up behind you . . . and this particular intruder had sneaked up very close behind him indeed. Steed's finely-tuned senses could detect a large man, a matter of inches from his back.

Thought turned into action. A precise, fluid action. Steed rammed his cue backwards as hard and fast as he could, judging it to be about the right height for a man's groin.

A shriek of agony told him he had judged well. Spinning round. Steed confronted the pain-twisted face of Boris, coming down to a level with his own chest as the man doubled up in agony. Steed whirled the cue in his hands, spinning it round the opposite way. Forming a perfect bridge with his left hand, he lined up the heavy end of the cue and played a perfect shot . . . straight into the centre of Boris's temple. With a dull groan, the man crumpled, knocked senseless.

Steed looked down at him for a moment, then crossed to the door, calling down the corridor. 'Mike? Come here.'

Gambit ran all the way, sensing the urgency in Steed's voice. Entering the games room, he gazed down at the unconscious Boris in bewilderment. 'What happened?'

'I just potted a Red.' Steed indulged himself in a broad smile at his own joke. He laid his cue down on the table, bent down and grabbed Boris by his lapels. 'Help me drag him over to a chair.'

Together, they dragged the heavy man across the room and lifted him into one of Steed's leather armchairs. Steed slapped the man's face several times.

Boris groaned, moved his head sluggishly, and his eyes flickered open.

'All right. What do you want?' Steed snapped. 'Why were you creeping up behind me?'

Boris groaned again, reaching up a hand to his throbbing head. 'I didn't want to spoil your shot,' he slurred thickly.

'Very considerate of you,' Steed shot back sarcastically. 'Thoughtful . . . but stupid. And painful. Now what are you doing here, Boris?'

'It's Olga. She wants to see you. Tonight,' Boris volunteered. 'It's very urgent.'

'Where?'

'At the Embassy. Nine o'clock.'

Steed considered, and made a decision. 'All right. I'll be there.' He turned to Gambit. 'Get him out of here, Mike.' A sudden thought struck him. 'Where's Spence?'

Gambit shrugged. 'He hasn't shown up yet. It's not like old Spence to be late for an appointment. He was so insistent we got together this morning as well.'

Steed shook his head in puzzlement. 'There's something funny going on, I know it.' He jerked his head down at Boris once again. 'See him out of the grounds, Mike, then phone Purdey and get her out here. I have a feeling we're in for some action today.'

'Right.' Gambit dragged Boris to his feet and supported the stumbling man to the door. Their footsteps faded away down the corridor.

Steed sank down into the vacated armchair to think.

His sense of uneasiness was no longer a vague one. Now, he sensed trouble. Big trouble.

But what? That was, indeed, the question.

Bill Spencer arrived nearly forty minutes late, offering no word of explanation or apology. Steed greeted him warmly, clapping him on his broad back. 'Spence. It's good to see you, after such a long time. How are you keeping?'

Spencer's head turned slowly, unnaturally. He stared blankly into Steed's face, as though he did not recognize the friend he had known for nearly fifteen years. His grey eyes were strangely vacant and unblinking.

For a second his lips trembled slightly, as though he were about to speak. The rest of his face remained impassive. Then, without any attempt at greeting, he ignored Steed completely and turned back to Gambit. 'I do not have much time. Shall we get on with it?' he snapped in a tense voice.

Gambit and Steed exchanged a quick, puzzled glance. The man was not himself at all. In all the years they had known Bill Spencer, he had always been the master of the amusing anecdote, the quick witticism. They had often marvelled that a man with such a gentle and unembittered sense of humour could become such a deadly fighting machine at a moment's notice.

Steed nodded his head, almost imperceptibly. Gambit was quick to get the message. 'Right, let's go, Spence. A quick game of squash first, to warm up?'

'If you insist,' Spencer agreed grudgingly, following him towards the gymnasium.

Steed watched them go, his face drawn with worry. There were too many strange things happening too fast for peace of mind. Instinct, and an innate urge for survival, told him that they must all tread warily until the situation started to reveal itself. No doubt his little meeting with Olga Perinkov would help to shed some light on the matter.

Pondering over the possibilities, Steed strolled out into the grounds, with the vague idea of walking around to the gymnasium windows, where he could perhaps learn a little more by studying Bill Spencer's odd behaviour without being observed himself. Stepping out through the front door, Steed began to walk stealthily around the west wing of the big house. He skirted the shrubbery, stepping gingerly over his beds of prize azalias and pressed himself close to the wall. Quietly, he crept along it towards the gymnasium windows.

A faint drumming sound came to his ears. Steed, his ears attuned to all possible equestrian noises, quickly identified it as the sound of a rapidly-approaching horse being hard-ridden over rough country.

He backed away from the window as quietly as he had approached it, retracing his steps to the front door. Gazing out past the hay-barn into the open fields beyond his own land, he picked out the approaching rider, eating up the distance at a dangerously fast gallop.

Steed recognized David Milner by his riding style long before the man's face was clearly visible. A little too detached to be called a close friend, yet sociable enough to be more than a mere business acquaintance, Steed had known Milner for some years. A successful estate agent, Milner had been responsible for Steed's acquisition of his current property at a remarkably reasonable price. From Steed's satisfaction and gratitude, and from the consuming love of horses and the Turf which both men shared, had grown their tenuous relationship.

Milner's known love for horses puzzled Steed as he watched the man reach the perimeter of his land. It was uncharacteristic of the man to push a horse so recklessly over open ground. On top of that, Milner was not the sort of individual usually given to rush, or panic . . . a state which his current rate of approach would appear to indicate. Normally, Milner was a slow, methodical man, with an alert mind which applied cold logic to virtually every problem, and whose mind functioned with the unemotional precision of a pocket calculator.

Milner hardly reined in his mount at all as he thundered round the outbuildings and headed directly for Steed's gravel drive. Small stones showered into the air as the black mare's hooves smashed into the loose surface.

Steed stepped forward to greet his unexpected visitor, reaching out with his right hand to grasp the horse's bridle. As Milner reined the animal in with unnatural ferocity, Steed smiled up at him. 'Nice to see you, David. What's the great hurry?'

Milner interrupted tersely, dismissing Steed's attempt at social courtesy. 'Came to warn you, Steed,' he managed to gasp out. 'You're in terrible danger.'

Milner straightened in the saddle as he prepared to dismount. The movement, fluid and natural, was suddenly wrong. Milner stiffened and jerked as his left leg came up and over his mount's flank. With his right foot still in the stirrup, Milner seemed to go limp, sliding down out of the saddle to collapse on the ground.

Steed stooped at once, quickly disengaging Milner's foot from the stirrup and placing one hand behind the man's back to help him to his feet. His fingers encountered something warm, and sticky to the touch. It was a sensation Steed was too familiar with. Withdrawing his hand, he looked at the crimson bloodstains on his fingers with the faintest shudder of distaste.

Shielded by the horse, Steed raised his hand to his forehead and stared out across the open countryside. His keen eyes picked up the faintest glint of light as the sun bounced off the front lens of a telescopic rifle sight for a fraction of a second. Steed saw the faint shape of a man crawl away down the other side of a high hill, less than a kilometre away. Near enough to kill, but too far away to chase. Satisfied the assassin had departed, Steed bent over the body of David Milner. He was dead. The gunman, whoever he was, knew how to make sure of his kill. The high-velocity bullet had taken Milner in the back, placed perfectly to penetrate right through to his heart.

A distinctive buff-coloured envelope protruded from Milner's top pocket. Steed recognized it somehow, without being able to quite place where he had seen its twin before. Gingerly, he slipped the envelope out and investigated its contents.

Two halves of an ordinary card tumbled out. The King of Hearts. Steed held one half in either hand, his eyes flicking from one to another alternately. His gaze dropped to the dead body of David Milner. 'The King is dead . . . long live the King,' Steed muttered under his breath. He turned the half-cards over, further mystified to see his own name printed on one of them in large black capitals.

With a sudden mental jolt, Steed recalled where and when he had seen that buff envelope before. Bill Spencer had been carrying one. Steed had noticed it earlier, sticking out of the right-hand pocket of the man's black leather jacket.

A strange coincidence. Two old friends, both suddenly fired with the urge to drop in unexpectedly. Both acting strangely out of character. Both men carrying buff envelopes. One of them had brought death.

Pushing the chain of coincidence one stage further, Steed realized that Mike Gambit was in deadly danger. Galvanized into action, he sprinted into the house, heading for the gymnasium.

In the changing room, Bill Spencer's jacket was hung neatly on a peg, the mysterious envelope plainly visible. Steed extracted it quickly, upending it and tipping its contents on to the hard wooden bench. Another card, cut in half . . . this time the Jack of Hearts. Without having to turn them over, Steed knew which name would be printed on one of them. He did so anyway; staring at Gambit's name morosely.

The door to the gymnasium was locked from the inside, just as Steed had expected. He pressed his mouth to the keyhole. 'Mike, are you all right?'

Gambit's voice came back, noticeably short of breath. 'Fine, Steed. Old Spence is sure putting the pressure on though.'

Steed shouted. 'Watch him.' He moved back, away from the door and raised his right foot. Summoning every ounce of his strength, he kicked out at it. The lock burst open, and Steed sprang into the room.

Gambit turned in surprise, his mouth falling open, 'Steed, what in God's name . . .'

The sentence ended in a painful gasp of indrawn breath as Spencer took quick advantage of his opponent's distraction to deliver a vicious flying toe-kick to his kidneys.

Surprised, winded, but acting instinctively, Gambit absorbed the blow as best he could and rolled sideways across the mat, springing up into a half-crouch.

Spencer had not even appeared to notice Steed's dramatic entrance. His attention was firmly upon Gambit. He moved forward with the predatory precision of a killer upon his prey. Whirling, he lashed out with another high kick, aimed at Gambit's throat. Gambit weaved sideways, dodging the kick with a look of shocked surprise upon his face. He knew enough about the martial arts to realize that such a kick was an intended killer, banned by mutual agreement in any friendly sparring bout.

Steed called again, 'He's trying to kill you, Mike.'

Gambit moved away, warily. 'Don't understand, Steed.'

'Neither do I . . . yet. Just bring him down, stun him.'

Desperate although the contest already was, Gambit managed a thin smile. 'Easier said than done, old son. Like I said, Spence is really putting on the pressure.'

He circled his opponent, searching out an opening for an aggressive attack. Spencer, past master at his killing craft, kept well out of striking distance.

Gambit decided to go in anyway. It was a clever trap. Spencer seemed to be just within range as Gambit jumped forward, his extended knuckles seeking a target just under the man's ribs. Without appearing to move, Spencer weaved back a matter of centimetres, so that Gambit's weight threw him slightly off balance when the blow failed to connect. The attack was instantly countered. Spencer pivoted on the balls of his feet, his left arm slicing up into the air and down again with the speed of a striking snake. The rock-like edge of his hand cracked down across Gambit's wrist, drawing a cry of pain. Gambit moved back, nursing the bruised bone and counting on his footwork to keep him clear of further trouble. His movements lacked their normal fluidity. Steed, watching anxiously, could see that the stilted, awkward motion was that of a wounded animal. Gambit was on the defensive, in serious trouble.

Spencer realized it too. It was time to go in for the kill. Delving into his fighting suit, he withdrew a gleaming bayonet from his belt. With a loud cry of triumph, he jumped high into the air, his body flying sideways. Landing a good two feet nearer his opponent, Spencer's whole body seemed to extend itself as though it were made of india-rubber. The wicked point of the bayonet came round in a sweeping, disembowelling arc across Gambit's unprotected belly.

Gambit's knees snapped forward, his body doubling. The bayonet sailed harmlessly past, just catching a loose fold of his suit and shredding the rough cotton with a faint zip.

The bayonet flipped in the air as Spencer tossed it from one hand to the other. His lightning fingers closed around the hilt and thrust it forward in one continuous, smooth movement. This time, Gambit had no room for manoeuvre left. The sharp point pierced his suit, just above the hip. Falling back, he started down in disbelief as a crimson stain bubbled out through the crisp whiteness of his suit.

Steed bent to the floor of the gymnasium as Spencer changed the bayonet back to his right hand and moved in to finish it all off. He scooped a heavy medicine ball up in both hands, bending his back and throwing all his weight and momentum into hurling it at Spencer's back.

The ball landed between Spencer's broad shoulder-blades, throwing him forward with a greater force and speed than his legs could compensate for. As he dived, head-first towards the mat, Gambit ran forward, his right foot lashing out towards the man's face.

The blow connected . . . hard. Stunned, Spencer collapsed limply on to his stomach. As he landed, heavily, there was a brief, bloodcurdling scream of agony. He lay very still.

Steed stepped over, bending down and grasping the man by the shoulder to flip him over. Spencer's body came away from the mat with a glutinous, sucking sound.

Steed's eyes flickered from the glistening pool of fresh blood on the mat to the bayonet buried deep in Spencer's belly. The man had fallen straight on to it, the weight of his burly body thrusting it in up to the hilt.

Steed cursed under his breath. Another playing card – another dead man. Whatever this new card game was, it was a deadly one.

. . . And somebody else held all the trumps.

There was silence for a while. Finally, clutching one hand over his slow-bleeding wound, Gambit spoke. 'What the hell is going on, Steed?'

'Snap, perhaps?' he observed grimly. 'I have another dead man outside.'

CHAPTER 5

The three sat around Steed's conference table. Spread out in front of them were the two dissected playing cards, two pieces of paper marked with a cross to symbolize the two dead men, and three empty notebooks. He looked at his two companions in turn, hopefully.

'So, what have we actually got?' Steed murmured.

'Problems?' Purdey suggested brightly, quickly withering under Steed's sardonic gaze.

'The cards are obviously some kind of code, or signal,' Gambit put in. 'One assumes that each half-card holder has a specific task to perform upon receipt of the missing half.'

Steed nodded. 'A fairly logical deduction,' he agreed. 'Question one: exactly what are these tasks, and question two: who is giving the orders?'

'Two questions, no answers,' Purdey said quietly. 'We're not doing very well, are we?'

Steed opened his mouth to say something scathing, then changed his mind. Purdey did have a good point.

'What about your meeting with Olga tonight?' Gambit asked. 'Do you think she is going to supply any of the answers?'

Steed shrugged. 'I don't know. Perhaps. Somehow, I feel that she is after some extra information herself. Maybe she wants to know how much we know. Don't forget that she is in direct touch with the Central Commissariat. They should know what's going on, if anyone does. I'd like to have a few more pieces of this jigsaw filled in before I go and see her.'

'So where do we start?' Gambit asked.

'David Milner was married,' Steed answered. 'I suggest we start with his wife, Suzy. Purdey – take a car and see if you can bring her back here. It's a long shot, but she may know what her husband was involved in.'

'Right.' Purdey stood up, preparing to leave the room. She stopped by the door. 'If I can't persuade her to come back here? Or can't find her?'

'Do what you can,' Steed said, not very helpfully. He turned back to Gambit as she left, closing the door quietly behind her. 'Meanwhile, I suggest we glean what we can from Spencer's record. There might, conceivably, be some sort of clue in that.'

'I'll get it.' Gambit rose, crossing the study to Steed's private files and sorting through the dozens of thick dossiers. Extracting Bill Spencer's file, he brought it back to the conference table and laid it down. Steed shuffled the papers out on the table and began to study them.

'How long was he working as official instructor for us?' Gambit wanted to know.

'Ten years,' Steed answered, checking the papers in front of him. 'And for three years before that, he was in the Hong Kong police force.'

'And before that?'

'Before that, we can't really be sure,' Steed murmured. 'Everybody he mentions as a personal reference are dead now . . . natural causes, I might add. The company he says he worked with for six years went bankrupt and out of business. He went to a private school which burnt down a few years after he left, and both his parents died when he was eighteen.'

'It smells,' Gambit muttered.

Steed nodded. 'A faint aroma of fish, I must agree. 'But only faint. All these facts could be absolutely correct. Thirteen years is a long time. People *do* die, companies *do* go out of business.'

'And schools burn down,' Gambit added, with a tinge of sarcasm. 'It happens all the time. Damned conveniently, too.'

Steed stood up and crossed to his files. 'There's one other odd thing,' he murmured distantly, pulling out a single sheet of paper and carrying it back to the table. He thrust it under Gambit's nose. 'Here's a list of the personnel Spencer trained personally. Take a look.'

Gambit's eyes flicked through the list of names. He pursed his lips, letting out a low whistle. 'Very impressive,' he muttered. 'But what's odd about it?'

Steed sucked at the inside of his cheek, pensively. 'Just that Bill Spencer was so good. He was the best unarmed combat instructor there was. That list of names testifies to that. Bill Spencer was probably the finest human fighting machine outside the Orient.'

'So?'

'So he knew far too much to fall on that blade when I hit him with the medicine ball,' Steed said quietly. 'Spence must have had a thousand tricks to avoid that. His normal reflexes were more than fast enough to have discarded the bayonet before he fell.'

'What exactly are you suggesting?' Gambit asked. 'That Spencer deliberately turned that bayonet on himself. He committed suicide?'

'That's exactly what I'm saying,' Steed answered. 'I think it is glaringly obvious. In the split second that Spencer realized he had failed in his task, he self-destructed, just like a machine.'

'Wow!' Gambit said, getting the message. 'So we're up against a suicide squad.'

'It certainly looks like it. Whoever is giving the orders is utterly ruthless. Human life means absolutely nothing at all.' He paused, to let his words sink in. 'Which brings us to another suicide . . . and another coincidence,' he said, after a while.

'Perov?' Gambit volunteered.

'Perov,' Steed said, firmly. 'A tenuous connection, I admit, but I don't think we can afford to overlook any possibilities at this stage.'

'Which might explain why Olga Perinkov is worried,' Gambit suggested, now building up on Steed's conjecture. 'If Perov's death was some sort of starting signal for an extermination campaign, she'd want to know if there's some sort of double-play going on behind her back.'

'Exactly,' Steed said. 'And Nikolai Perov was the master of the double-play. He practically invented the game.'

The roar of a high-powered car coming up the drive interrupted the two men's discussion. They heard the car screech to a halt with a hiss of flying gravel, and female footsteps climbing the front steps. The front door opened and closed.

Purdey knocked, briefly on the study door before entering. She was alone.

'Milner's wife?' Steed asked, glancing up.

'Gone,' Purdey said simply. 'In rather a hurry, I should say. A few of her clothes are gone, the rest are scattered around the bedroom. Any woman who would treat de Quincy originals in that fashion is in a terrible hurry, or a full-scale panic.'

'Any ideas?' Gambit asked. 'Any clue at all as to where the bird might have flown.'

'Or been taken,' Steed put in. 'We mustn't overlook that possibility.'

Purdey shook her head. 'I don't think so. There was no evidence of any kind of a struggle. Just panic.'

'Well,' Steed asked, impatiently. 'Were there any pointers as to where she might have gone?'

'Only this.' Purdey produced a small framed photograph and a sheaf of loose snapshots. She handed the frame to Steed.

It showed a smiling David and Suzy Milner standing outside a small country cottage, with a rose trellis above the doorway. In the background was a small church, with an ornately-decorated steeple.

Gambit, looking over Steed's shoulder, was unimpressed. 'Don't see how that's going to be any help.'

Purdey flashed him a contemptuous glance. 'Idiot. It means that the Milners owned a country cottage. I'll bet ten to one that's where she'll be hiding out.'

Gambit laughed. 'You women. No sense of logic whatsoever. That photograph is totally inconclusive. It doesn't mean they own a cottage at all. They may have rented it for a holiday at one time. Even more likely, it is the home they owned before moving here.'

Purdey refused to be shot down. 'Suzy Milner is wearing wave-pattern sandals,' she murmured with quiet confidence. 'They only came out last season. Trust a man to have no concept of fashion whatsoever.'

'They still could have rented it,' Gambit muttered, defensively.

'Nope.' Purdey held a couple of the loose snaps under his nose. Two of them showed the Milners in the garden of the same cottage, busy tending the garden. 'You don't cultivate the garden of a cottage unless you own it,' she said triumphantly. A crafty smile spread across her face. 'And that is more than just logical. I should say that was painfully obvious, even to an idiot.'

Gambit, much embarassed, refused to give up. 'There must be at least twenty million cottages in this country,' he observed, in a disgruntled tone.

Steed looked up from the photograph with a mildly rebuking grimace. 'Have you two finished bickering?'

'Sorry, Steed.' Gambit pulled himself together and bent over his colleague's shoulder again. 'Assuming that this cottage does exist, how do we set about tracking it down?'

'Roland,' Steed said, confidently. 'Roland the rose-freak.'

Gambit looked openly sceptical. 'I know he's an expert, but I don't see how he is going to identify a single cottage by the roses growing over the door.'

Steed flashed Gambit the sort of look usually reserved for backward children and minor civil servants. 'Not by the roses. By the steeple . . . the little church in the background.'

'Oh.' Gambit was even more mystified. 'I didn't know Roland was an authority on churches as well.'

'He isn't,' Steed said. 'At least, as far as I know, he isn't.'

'Then how?' Gambit asked, now thoroughly confused.

'The bishop,' Steed answered, making another abrupt mental jump which left his colleagues even further in the dark.

Gambit shook his head slowly. 'Steed, I'm just not with you,' he muttered, in a puzzled voice.

There was just the faintest trace of exasperation in Steed's tone when he spoke again. 'Roland's rose-growing friend, the bishop. He'll be able to tell us where that church is. I should say that steeple was quite unique.'

'Of course . . . the bishop,' Purdey put in, trying to score one last point. Gambit glared at her.

Steed ignored them both. He stood, crossing the study to the telephone and picking up the receiver. He dialled a number and waited for several seconds. 'Ah, Roland? It's John Steed. Listen Roland, could you get on the blower and get your friend the bishop round to your place? Yes, it's rather urgent. We'll be down in twenty minutes or so.'

He replaced the receiver and stood looking at Gambit and Purdey for a while. 'Well?'

'Well what?' Purdey asked.

Steed shook his head with a gesture of exasperation. 'Well, are we going to wait here all day?' He led the way outside to the car.

No-one came out to greet them as Gambit pulled the car to a halt outside the door of Roland's lodge house. The heady scent of hundreds of roses hung in the still, quiet air. Nothing moved. The gardens themselves seemed deserted.

Steed stepped out of the car. 'Roland,' he called. There was no answer. A worried frown crossed Steed's brow. Everything seemed quiet and peaceful . . . too peaceful. After the preceding events of the day, Steed felt rather apprehensive – with good cause. He called Roland's name out again, this time time in a louder voice. Still there was no reply. Steed turned to his companions. 'Mike, you go and take a look around the back of the house. Purdey – you have a roam around the gardens.'

As his colleagues set off, Steed approached the front door of the lodge house cautiously. It was slightly ajar. Steed edged along it, raising his foot to kick it fully open.

'Steed. Over here, quickly.' Purdey's voice sounded from the depths of the rose garden. Her voice was urgent, the tone grim.

Steed ran back down the steps, nearly cannoning into Gambit, who also came running around the other side of the house. Together, they raced to Purdey's side, stopping dead as they gazed along the line of her pointing, slightly trembling, finger.

Sticking out of a clump of rose bushes and surrounding shrubs were a pair of legs. They were deathly still.

Steed stepped forward gingerly, reaching out to part the overhanging foliage. Underneath, Roland lay full-length on his back, his eyes wide open and staring blankly upwards.

'It looks like we got here too late,' Steed murmured sadly. 'Poor old Roland.'

Purdey nodded in agreement. 'He was a bit of a nut about his roses . . . but I did like him,' she whispered. Her words jammed in her throat, caught in a bottleneck as a sudden scream ripped up from somewhere deep in her belly.

Steed's eyes opened wide as he gazed down. Roland's 'corpse' was moving! Slowly, soundlessly, one arm came up into the air. Roland's fist clenched, with index finger extended. Gently, he lay the finger across his lips. 'Shush,' Roland whispered, a little testily. Taking his finger away from his mouth, he prodded upwards, indicating a spot about two feet above his face.

Steed and his companions followed his direction, completely dumbfounded. Two roses, their heads buried into one another, were held in position by a small rubber band.

'They're mating,' Roland whispered, by way of explanation. 'It's a very rare and beautiful moment.'

Purdey laughed with relief. 'Must say I never thought of you as a Peeping Tom, Roland.'

Roland slithered out from his cover and scrambled quietly to his feet. 'It's no laughing matter,' he complained gently. 'Harvest Sunrise and Bates's Joy . . . brought together in union for the very first time. With luck, I could get an honorable mention in the Rose-Grower's Monthly.'

Steed wrapped one arm around the man's shoulders and led him gently away. 'Roland, can we get down to business?'

Roland regarded him with a puzzled, slightly pitying expression. He could never quite understand how any normal human being could fail to share his passion for the most beautiful of all growing things. 'Of course, Steed. What can I do for you?'

'Where's your friend, the bishop?' Steed wanted to know.

Roland jerked his head towards the house. 'In my study, guzzling my best port if I know the old devil at all. He's a little bit sensitive about this forced mating, y'know. Thinks it's all a bit too modern, too permissive, if you know what I mean.'

Steed allowed himself a thin smile. 'Quite.' He steered Roland towards the house. As they walked, he pulled the playing cards from his pocket. 'Mean anything to you?'

Roland took the halved cards and studied them for a few seconds. 'Playing cards, cut in half,' he ventured.

Steed nodded. 'Obviously. But I think they mean something. One of these cards preceded a murder.'

'And the other one a near murder,' Gambit interjected. 'With me as the intended victim.'

'Dearie me.' Roland looked at the torn cards with fresh interest. 'Code cards, perhaps?'

'Something like that,' Steed said. 'Well? Does it bring anything to mind?'

Roland shook his head slowly. 'No, I don't think so.' Suddenly, his eyes widened. He clicked his fingers. 'Wait a minute. Now I come to think of it, there *was* something. It was a long time ago, though,' he finished, doubtfully.

'Go on,' Steed said, eagerly. 'What about the cards?'

Roland sucked his teeth as he struggled to remember. 'Ooh, it must be all of twelve years ago,' he muttered at last. 'At least that. There was only an unconfirmed rumour . . . very vague, you understand. Something to do with old Perov . . . some master-plan which took him out of circulation for a couple of years. No-one in the department knew where he had gone to ground, or what he was up to . . . it was even rumoured that he'd been bumped off. He wasn't of course.'

Steed interrupted. 'Get to the point, Roland.'

'Well, eventually we found out that he *was* up to something,' Roland went on. 'It was code-named "House of Cards".'

Steed smiled with relief. 'Now we're getting somewhere. Well, what exactly was this master-plan?'

Roland's face fell. 'That's it, Steed . . . we never found out. Perov really put the shutters up on that one. Whatever it was, it was top security and incredibly devious. We lost three men without even getting the faintest whiff of what was going on.'

A look of disappointment crossed Steed's face. 'Oh. So we're still in the dark?'

Roland nodded sadly. 'Afraid so, Steed. You know what Perov was like. Too damned devious by half.'

'Yes.' Steed could only sigh in agreement. They reached the front steps of the house.

'Anyway, come in and meet the bishop,' Roland said, changing the subject. 'And have a drink, if the old rogue has left a bottle in the house.' He led them in through the front door and down the hallway towards his study.

The bishop turned, a guilty look upon his ruddy face,

as they entered. Ruefully, he began to place the port decanter back on the shelf.

'Do help yourself, Bishop,' Roland offered. 'Some friends of mine would like to have a word with you.'

The bishop beamed, lifting the decanter again and selecting a large crystal goblet. 'Really shouldn't, of course . . . but you do keep such an excellent cellar, my dear Roland.' He filled the glass to its brim, then turned to face his visitors. Roland made the formal introductions, escorting the cleric to a large white leather chesterfield.

Steed wasted no time. He sat down beside the bishop, thrusting the framed photograph into his spare hand. 'Recognize anything?'

'By Jove, yes,' the man muttered enthusiastically. 'Queen's Poacher.'

'Queen's Poacher?' Steed repeated, blankly. 'Where's that?'

The Bishop prodded the photograph. 'Right there, my dear fellow. Growing over the door. Terribly pruned, I might add. Fellow ought to be dunked in weed-killer.'

Steed heaved a small sigh of exasperation. He was getting rather tired of the way in which every conversation seemed to end with some variety of rose. He stabbed his finger at the church and steeple in the background. 'I was thinking more in terms of that,' he urged.

'Ah, yes. Ugly monstrosity, isn't it? Late Saxon, by the look of those cornices.'

'But where is it?' Steed pressed, his impatience mounting.

'Oh, nowhere around here, I'm afraid,' the bishop answered casually. 'Not even in my diocese in fact. A little village named Wentlock, if my memory serves. Eight or nine miles outside Epsom.'

Steed breathed a sigh of relief. 'Thank you, Bishop. You've been a great help.'

That topic of conversation seemingly exhausted, the bishop returned to his own pet subject. 'You're not a rose man then, Mr Steed?'

Steed smiled politely, flashing urgent messages in Gambit's direction. 'No, I'm afraid not.'

'Alas, I must myself admit to being a helpless addict,' the bishop droned on. 'I admit it to my undying disgrace. Many is the time when I have found myself preoccupied with the voracity of greenfly when I should be tending my human flock. Sinfully preoccupied, I fear.' He pressed a hand on to Steed's arm, steering him toward's the port decanter.

Steed looked over hopelessly as Gambit hurried to his rescue. 'Mike, take Purdey and get down there right away,' Steed hissed. 'I want as much information as you can dig up. I'll meet you back at the farm this evening.'

'Right,' Gambit said. 'What are you going to do?'

Steed groaned under his breath. 'I rather think I am going to talk about roses,' he said glumly. He rolled his eyes expressively as the bishop towed him away.

'Yes Steed, a man who knows roses is a man who knows God in his most creative moments, I always say. Take the fragile purity of "Peace", for example . . .'

Steed watched Gambit and Purdey leave out of the corner of his eye, before wearily surrendering himself to the inevitable.

'. . . As a man of God, I find it hard to spread my love of all living creatures far enough to take in slugs,' the bishop prattled on.

Steed glanced at his watch. 'Good Heavens, is that the time?' he said, with mock concern. 'I really must be going.' He managed to detach himself for long enough to seek out Roland. 'Roland, I must get back. Can you lay on a car?'

Roland grinned, nodding imperceptibly at his other guest. 'Lovely old chap, but he does go on a bit, doesn't he?'

'To say the least,' Steed agreed fervently.

'I'll go and find Frederick,' Roland announced. 'He's about somewhere. He'll drive you home.'

'Thanks,' Steed said gratefully. Roland strode towards the door. Steed fixed a sickly smile on his face as the bishop closed in again. 'The Hertfordshire Maiden, now . . . *there's* a bloom to stir the hearts of mortal men . . .'

The man's words tumbled over the top of Steed's head in a verbal blur. His thoughts were on more serious topics. They were suddenly shattered by a loud cry from outside.

For a big man, the bishop moved extremely swiftly. Girding his skirt about him, he beat Steed to the door by a good six feet, racing into the garden, and round the corner of a high yew hedge, from behind which came the sounds of a violent struggle.

Steed ran around the hedge just in time to see the bishop delivering a booted and gaitered kick which would have put many a karate expert to shame. The blow connected full in the face of Frederick, Roland's private chauffeur, who was sitting astride his employer's chest, pinning him to the ground.

Soundlessly, Frederick fell back, out cold.

Steed looked down at Roland in alarm. 'Are you all right?'

Roland pushed himself to his feet shakily. His face was grey. Blood gushed from two nasty wounds in his throat. 'Yes, I think so,' he muttered, his voice trembling. 'I don't know what came over the man. He just went for me . . . tried to cut my damned jugular vein with a pair of my best pruning shears.'

Steed looked at Roland's wounds. 'He wasn't far out,' he observed. 'If it hadn't been for the bishop here, you would have been a goner.'

The bishop gave a little whoop of joy. 'Glory be. I have smitten down a sinner,' he cried exultantly. 'A violent criminal, addicted to the vice of gambling.'

'Gambling?' Steed followed the bishop's nod down towards the ground by Frederick's hand. Beside the bloodstained secateurs lay a torn playing card. The nine of Hearts.

'I don't know what could have come over him . . . some sort of brainstorm, a mental aberration,' Roland was muttering, still shaken. 'Frederick has been with me for years.'

Steed turned to the battling bishop. 'Bishop, would you be so good as to help Roland into the house and try to stop the bleeding?' he asked. 'I'll take care of this fellow.'

'Of course, old chap.' The bishop threw his arm under Roland's shoulders and began assisting him towards the house, muttering soothing words of comfort. 'Lucky for you he didn't push you down on to those Wheatcroft Wonders. Would have done for them, that's for sure.'

Steed bent over the unconscious Frederick, pocketing the two halves of the card before dragging the man unceremoniously by the collar.

Frederick was conscious, yet not conscious. Steed was puzzled. The man had long since come to, yet he acted as though he were in some kind of coma. His eyes were glazed and unblinking, his mouth slackly open. Even his breathing was too shallow to be called normal. He sat, tied in a chair, as still as a dead man.

Steed glanced up at Roland, whose neck was swathed in bandages. 'What do you make of it, Roland?'

The man shook his head in puzzlement, wincing slightly at the pain it caused him. 'Damned if I know, Steed. It's as though he were in a hypnotic trance, or something like that.'

'Catatonic, not hypnotic,' the bishop volunteered coming over to join them. He cast a knowing glance at the rigid man in the chair. 'Yes, I should say definitely catatonic.'

Steed was impressed. 'You've seen this sort of thing before, bishop?'

The cleric nodded. 'Oh yes. Frequently. In my earlier days, out in Africa . . . came across it all the time, y'know. Self-induced, sometimes . . . either from chewing too much dagga-weed, or from ritual dances. More often it was brought about by witch-doctors usually as some form of punishment. Conditioned to it, you see, these primitives.'

Roland glanced at Steed questioningly. 'Could it be a post-conditioning state?'

'It fits,' Steed muttered, non-committally. 'Bill Spencer was definitely under some kind of compulsion. Frederick here too, from the look of it. Somehow, the card triggers them off to perform a set function – so far to kill a specific person. If they're stopped, they just seem to switch off, like machines.'

'But how?' Roland wanted to know.

Steed shrugged. 'Who knows? Some degree of psychic conditioning . . . drugs . . . narco-hypnosis . . . sensory deprivation . . . neuro-surgery . . . take your pick. There are a dozen nasty ways to interfere with the human mind.'

'Are you going to try to question him?' Roland asked, pointing to his chauffeur.

Steed shook his head. 'I don't think there's much point. He won't talk. He won't do anything. He'll just sit there and die, eventually.'

Roland's voice was horror-struck. 'My God, Steed, what are we up against?'

'That,' Steed replied flatly, 'Is a very good question.'

CHAPTER 6

Suzy Milner was near the point of hysteria. The interior of the cottage, with all doors and windows closed and bolted, was stiflingly hot. The white telephone, all day promising a reassuring call from David, remained silent. The heat, the silence, and the fear had taken their toll of her taut nerves. She sat, rocking herself slightly in a wicker chair, cradling a twelve-bore shotgun across her knees and staring out through the net curtains into the front garden and the road beyond.

Gambit slewed Steed's car to a halt outside the the front gate. Suzy Milner stiffened in the chair, her fingers clenching around the butt and barrel of the shotgun until her knuckles turned white. She sensed menace in the sudden arrival of these two strangers – danger in the urgency of their exit from the car and their progress up the path towards the front door.

Instinctively, Suzy Milner thrust the heavy twin barrels through the window-pane, her finger already curled around the trigger.

Purdey, her senses finely attuned to the first signs of danger, picked up the first tinkle of shattering glass. 'Dive,' she screamed at Gambit, throwing herself aside even as the single word passed through her lips.

Gambit, his own actions equally primed, acted upon her warning without any hesitation at all. He hurled himself down towards the ground, executing a perfect forward roll which took him off the path and into a thick patch of shrubbery.

Both barrels of the shotgun boomed out, sending a withering cone of flying lead into the empty space both of them had occupied only a split second previously. Both Purdey and Gambit were on their feet again and sprinting for more solid cover before the faint click of the breech being opened came to their ears. Gambit threw himself down behind a low, but comfortingly stout brick wall. Purdey, heading across the small lawn towards the house, chose the cover of a stone statuette of a naked water-nymph, mounted on a heavy concrete pedestal. As they settled down, they heard the faint sound of two fresh shells being slipped into place, and the deliberate snap of the breech being closed again. The twin muzzles pointed out of the broken window once more.

Without sticking her head into sight, Purdey called towards the cottage. 'Mrs Milner? Suzy? We're friends... friends of David. We just want to talk to you.'

By way of an answer, Suzy Milner swung the shotgun round and blasted off one shot. Glancing up, Purdey saw the right arm of the statuette dissolve into a grey powder. Stone chippings showered down into her hair.

Gambit called across, urgently. 'You all right, Purdey?'

She managed a weak laugh. 'Fine Mike. Now I know how the Venus de Milo came into being.'

Suzy Milner squeezed the trigger again. This time, the hail of shot took the statuette's head clean off. Gambit and Purdey waited, listening intently as Suzy Milner reloaded yet again. It seemed she meant business, and wasn't short of spare ammunition.

'Believe us, Mrs Milner . . . we've come to help,' Gambit called.

The words were hardly out of his mouth than shot peppered off the top of the wall which sheltered him.

Purdey recognized the signs of a distraught, panicky female. Her reactions were too nervous, too quick. She hissed over at Gambit. 'It's no use, Mike, I don't think she's in any fit state to be rational. Talking won't do any good at all.'

There was a momentary silence as Gambit digested this information and considered other possibilities. Finally, he called back, softly. 'There's only one up the spout, old girl. If you can draw it off, I should be able to make it to the cottage before she reloads.'

Purdey thought about it, nodding to herself. It was the only way. Reaching out gingerly, she cupped her hands around the shattered head of the statuette, weighing it experimentally in the palm of her hand. Risking a quick peep over the top of the concrete pedestal, she took quick aim and then hurled the hunk of stone in a quick over-arm motion towards the cottage window.

Her aim was true. The missile sped to its target, shattering the remaining glass in the window. Suzy Milner pulled the trigger instinctively, loosing off her remaining cartridge harmlessly into the air.

Before the echo of the shot had quite died, Gambit had broken from his cover and was running in long, loping strides towards the cottage. Purdey looked up, her breath tight in her throat as he ate up the intervening space.

Ten yards from the house, she heard the sound of the first shell slipping into place. Eight yards . . . six, five. The second shell went into place. When Gambit was less than a yard from the shattered window, Purdey heard the loud click of the breech. Gambit had just failed to make it, by precious seconds. Purdey closed her eyes instinctively, expecting to see his running body blasted into a gory mess.

It was a pity. She missed the sheer poetry of movement as Gambit left the ground at the run, throwing himself head-first through the broken window with his arms bunched up around his face.

After the crashing and splintering of wood and the remaining pieces of glass came a brief and muted sound of a strictly one-sided struggle. Then there was silence.

Purdey opened her eyes to see the shotgun dropping out through the demolished window frame, quickly followed by Gambit's smiling face. 'All right now, sweetheart. Mrs Milner is at home to guests.'

'I'll just make myself presentable.' Purdey scrambled to her feet, dusting herself down. With as much dignity as she could muster, she strolled across the lawn towards the cottage.

Gambit opened the front door. Purdey walked in briskly, following him through to the small, sparsely-furnished living room. Her gaze fell upon Suzy Milner, collapsed, sobbing, on the floor. Purdey raised her eyes to meet Gambit's, jerking her head very slightly towards the kitchen door. 'Leave her to me, Mike. Why don't you be a real help and go and make us all a nice cup of tea?'

Gambit smiled. 'Thanks,' he murmured without malice, already sloping off to leave the two women together.

Purdey bent over the distraught Suzy, helping her gently to her feet. 'It's all right now,' she murmured soothingly. 'Just as I told you, we're friends of David's. We came here to help you.'

Suzy Milner choked back her tears, recovering herself. When Purdey had helped her to her chair, she looked up through moist eyes. 'He's dead, isn't he? David's dead?'

Purdey nodded sadly. 'I'm afraid so.'

A fresh tremor shook Suzy Milner's body, but she fought against it bravely. 'I knew,' she muttered bitterly. 'I knew the moment that message came for him this morning.'

'Tell me about the message,' Purdey prompted gently. 'It was a card, wasn't it? A torn playing card?'

Suzy Milner nodded. 'The King of Hearts. David had the other half locked away in his desk.'

'You knew about the card, then?'

Suzy nodded. 'I came across it by accident once... I was clearing up. It was such an odd thing to have locked away, so I asked David about it.'

Purdey listened sympathetically. It seemed best to let Suzy Milner speak at random, rather than press her for direct answers. That way, she might gain more precious information.

'At first, David flew into a rage,' Suzy went on. 'Accused me of prying into his private affairs. It was so untypical of him... he was like a man possessed. Then, when he calmed down a bit, he told me that one day, he might have to go back to a job he had never finished... that it might involve us both in danger. It was then that he bought this cottage... he called it our "safe place". He said that if ever the card came, he would have to go back to work. That I must run immediately, come here. He taught me to use the gun... said I must be prepared to defend, even to kill if anyone followed me here.'

Purdey interrupted her rambling flow of words discreetly. 'This unfinished work David spoke of . . . did he ever say what it was exactly?'

Suzy Milner shook her head. 'He wouldn't say. He just said that it would probably never happen . . . not after so long. He said that meeting me had changed the whole purpose of his life.'

Gambit came in from the kitchen bearing a tray of freshly-made tea. He had been listening intently to every word. He handed Suzy Milner a cup which she accepted with trembling fingers. 'Whoever killed your husband must not be allowed to go free, Mrs Milner,' he murmured quietly. 'That's why we are here. That's why you must tell us everything you know – the slightest clue you can think of, no matter how irrelevant or trivial it might seem. Do you understand?'

Suzy Milner nodded. 'I think so. Somehow, I trust you.'

'Good. Now think carefully. When David spoke about this unfinished work . . . did he ever say why it *was* unfinished?'

Suzy Milner concentrated for several seconds. 'He did make a sort of joke about it once. He said he had been retired early . . . put to sleep, I believe was the phrase he used. It seemed a funny thing to say.'

Gambit seized upon the word eagerly. 'Sleep? He said that word . . . sleep? Did he ever use the word "sleeper"?'

Suzy Milner shook her head. 'I don't think so. Why, does it mean something?'

Gambit nodded grimly, with a sideways glance at Purdey. 'Yes, I'm afraid it does, Mrs Milner. It means quite a lot.'

Purdey took over. 'How long have you known your husband, Mrs Milner?'

'Twelve years,' Suzy started to say, her voice breaking into a choked sob again. 'We were married only five weeks after we first met. We were very much in love.'

She broke off to gulp down the hot tea. Purdey waited patiently until she had recovered herself again.

'What about his friends . . . his relatives? Did you ever meet any of them?'

Again, Suzy Milner shook her head. 'David's parents were both dead. They were killed when Coventry was bombed, during the last war. He didn't seem to have many friends. He'd lost touch with all his old school pals because the school burned down . . . all the records were destroyed.'

Purdey looked at Gambit again. Their eyes met. Gambit nodded, showing that he had not missed the point.

'And his previous job? What did David do before he was an estate agent?' Purdey went on.

Suzy Milner shrugged. 'It was all a bit vague, really. David never wanted to talk about it. All I ever learned was that he had held an important post in a company which went bankrupt. I always got the feeling he was a little bitter about it.'

Again, Purdey and Gambit exchanged a knowing look. The picture was becoming all too clear . . . and familiar.

Purdey sighed deeply. She had hoped that Suzy Milner would be able to clear up a little of the mystery suurounding her late husband. As it was, she had told them virtually nothing. Purdey phrased her last question very carefully. 'Are you sure you never met anybody . . . anybody at all . . . who was in any way connected with David's life before you met him?'

'I'm sure,' Suzy Milner replied, firmly. She paused for a second, as though struck by a second thought. A slight frown creased her smooth brow. 'Wait. There was something odd once . . . someone we saw at a party somewhere . . .'

Purdey pressed in, eagerly. 'Yes, go on. What happened?'

Suzy Milner shook her head, uncertainly. 'It was nothing definite . . . just an odd feeling I got. Call it a woman's intuition if you like.'

Purdey smiled. 'Don't knock it, love, I never do.' She waited expectantly for the woman to continue.

'We were at this party,' Suzy Milner went on. 'David was acting normally . . . until he saw this woman come in. The minute he saw her, he started to tremble violently. I got the strong feeling that he knew her from the past . . . that she represented something nasty or unpleasant . . . even dangerous.'

'Go on,' Purdey said, excitely. It really seemed as though they might be getting somewhere at last.

'He denied ever seeing her before, of course,' Suzy continued. 'But he was on edge for the rest of the evening. He wouldn't go anywhere near this woman . . . he avoided her like the plague. I found that especially strange because her escort was a friend of his.'

'Who was the woman's escort?' Gambit put in.

The reply stunned them both. 'John Steed,' Suzy Milner said quietly.

Gambit looked at Purdey, a puzzled frown on his face. 'Tara King?' he muttered, doubtfully.

'Oh no, it wasn't Miss King,' Suzy Milner interrupted. 'I met her a couple of times. No, this woman was very tall, very elegant-looking. She was a redhead, I seem to remember. A very striking woman.'

Gambit and Purdey ran their memories back through the long list of Steed's past lady-loves. The same name sprang to both their lips in the same instant.

'Joanna,' Purdey said.

'Joanna Harrington,' Gambit agreed.

Suzy Milner shrugged. 'I didn't find out what her name was. We never saw her again.'

Gambit nodded distantly. 'Yes Steed was rather upset when she disappeared so suddenly. I think he was rather taken with her at the time.' He tapped Purdey on the shoulder. 'We'd better be getting back. Steed will want to know, now we have a name to work on.'

Purdey nodded, turning briefly to Suzy Milner. 'Will you be all right now?'

The woman nodded bravely. 'I'll be all right. Now that I know David won't be coming back, there's nothing to keep me here. I'll go down and stay with my sister in Torquay for a while. No-one can trace me there.'

'Good idea.' Purdey handed her a calling card. 'If anything else happens, or you remember anything else that could help us track down David's murderer, give me a ring at this number.'

'I will,' Suzy Milner promised. She stood up to escort them to the door. 'You will find him, won't you?'

'We'll get him . . . or her,' Gambit vowed. 'Your husband was a brave man.' He neglected to add that David Milner had also probably been an enemy agent at some time – very possibly a trained and practised assassin.

Suzy Milner closed the door quietly behind them

as Gambit and Purdey hurried down the drive and climbed into their car. She didn't wait to see them speed off.

Sixty yards further down the road, a dark blue Citroen snapped into life, pulling smoothly away from the verge to follow in their wake.

Gambit left the outskirts of the village a mile behind, cruising out into the open countryside. 'We have company,' he murmured, glancing in the rear-view mirror.

'We also have trouble,' Purdey muttered calmly, as the Citroen accelerated rapidly, zooming up behind them.

'Woman's intuition?' Gambit asked.

'Woman's eyesight,' Purdey shot back, pulling on Gambit's arm to direct his attention to the small, round bullet-hole which had just appeared in the rear side window.

Gambit's eyes darted back to the mirror as his toe poised ready to stamp down on the accelerator. Judging the speed of the approaching Citroen, he knew instinctively that flight was out of the question. Their pursuer was coming up too fast.

Instead, he shouted briefly at Purdey before changing his foot over the brake pedal instead. 'Duck – and brace yourself.' He crossed his arms over the padded steering wheel and jammed down hard on the brake.

The inertia-reel safety belts absorbed most of the shock as the car slewed off the road in a four-wheel skid and came to an abrupt halt. Gambit threw himself sideways, shielding Purdey's body in an instinctive act of gallantry. The Citroen screamed past, a hail of bullets cracking out above the roar of its engine.

It carried straight on, disappearing around a bend in the road without slowing up at all. Slowly, Purdey squirmed out from beneath her partner's body. 'Mike, this is so sudden,' she joked, a little nervously.

Gambit sat up, grinning wryly. 'I was just beginning to enjoy that,' he complained.

They both looked, somewhat apprehensively, at the road ahead.

'Think they'll come back for a second go?' Purdey asked.

'Want to wait here and find out?' Gambit answered.

Purdey shook her head. 'No way.'

'Right. Let's move.' Gambit threw open the car door and jumped out, running around the back of the vehicle to join Purdey as she scrambled out on her side. Together, they dived headlong into the deep, damp and rather smelly ditch beside the road. Heads tucked well down, they waited for several minutes. Nothing happened.

'Well, there's the answer,' Gambit said after a while, a trifle sheepishly. 'They're not coming back.'

Purdey stood up and started to clamber out of the ditch. Looking down, she moodily contemplated her muddy, spoiled clothes. '*Now* you tell me,' she muttered, with the faintest trace of real bitterness in her voice.

Gambit joined her on the road and walked around the car slowly, assessing the damage.

'Can you get her out of the ditch?' Purdey asked.

Gambit shrugged helplessly. 'Not a lot of point even trying,' he said, staring down at the offside wheels. Both tyres had been punctured by at least three bullets.

'So, what do we do now?' Purdey asked.

Gambit considered for a few seconds. 'I guess our best plan will be to walk down the road and try to find a telephone box,' he suggested. 'We can at least try to warn Steed, and let him know what's going on.'

Purdey shook her head doubtfully. 'I don't think that idea will serve much purpose,' she mused thoughtfully.

Gambit looked at her in surprise. 'What makes you say that?'

Purdey jerked her head down at the shredded tyres and the holes where other bullets had found their mark in the car's bodywork. 'All those shots were aimed low,' she pointed out. 'Therefore they weren't trying to kill us. If they'd wanted to do that they would have aimed higher.'

'So you think it was just a warning?'

Purdy shook her head again. 'More than that. I think they were just trying to stop us from getting back to Steed. The telephone is an obvious form of contact. Therefore whoever shot up the car will already have taken that into consideration . . . and have done something about it. Steed's telephone lines will have been cut.'

Gambit regarded her with quiet amazement. 'Whoever said that women have no sense of logic?' he murmured quietly. 'I just hope you're wrong, that's all.'

'I won't be,' Purdey said confidently, falling into step beside Gambit as he started to trudge up the deserted road.

There was a telephone kiosk about a quarter of a mile further up the road, just before a sharp bend. Gambit strode up to it, wrenched the door open and lifted the receiver, dialling Steed's number. The clear, continuous buzz of the unobtainable signal came over the line.

Purdey pulled open the kiosk door, stepping in beside him. She could tell by the exasperated frown on his face that she had been right. 'Told you,' she said simply as Gambit slammed the useless receiver back into its cradle.

'Well, little Miss Bright. What do you suggest we do now?' Gambit asked, just a little testily.

Purdey shrugged. 'You could try Roland's number, I suppose,' she answered, none too hopefully.

Gambit picked up the receiver and tried again. Once again, the receiver shrilled into his ear. 'They're pretty thorough,' he admitted grudgingly, starting to replace the telephone again.

'Correction. They're *very* thorough,' Purdey said in a strangely chilling voice. She tugged at Gambit's sleeve.

'I see what you you mean,' Gambit muttered resignedly, turning in response to Purdy's summons.

Outside the telephone kiosk, his heavy frame pressed against the door, stood Cartney. He had a Luger in his hand. Cartney tapped the silenced end of the gun's barrel on the glass of the kiosk. 'No sudden movements, please,' he murmured politely. 'Just raise your hands slowly into the air and press them against the side of the telephone box.'

While Gambit and Purdey did as they were told, Cartney fished in his pocket and pulled out a small metal cylinder. He raised it to his mouth, clenching his teeth around the wire pin which protruded from its side and jerking it free. Opening the kiosk door about two inches, he tossed the canister inside and pressed his full weight back against the door.

Gambit glanced down as the small cylinder rolled between his feet. It spluttered a couple of times, and then began to hiss. A greenish-brown smoke started to pour from the canister, swirling thickly around his ankles.

'Gas,' Gambit muttered.

'So what do we do now?' Purdey asked, fighting to keep panic from her voice.

Gambit flashed her an apologetic smile. 'Try not to breathe for about ten minutes?' he suggested, helpfully.

The gas quickly spread into a thick mist inside the closed confines of the telephone kiosk. Cartney smiled with satisfaction as his two victims slipped smoothly into unconsciousness, collapsing untidily upon the floor of the box. Satisfied that the gas grenade had done its work thoroughly, he stepped back, holding the door open until the gas dissipated into the open air. Only when the kiosk was completely clear again did he tuck the gun back in his pocket, bend down and begin to drag out the limp body of Gambit.

Just around the bend, Perov waited in the parked Citroen.

He nodded with satisfaction as Cartney carried the unconscious Purdey across and dumped her on the back seat with her companion.

'Excellent, excellent,' Perov muttered gleefully, rubbing his hands together. 'Everything is going splendidly . . . just as I planned.'

Cartney slipped into the driving seat and closed the car door. 'Where shall we take them?'

Perov's face became serious again. 'To the crematorium,' he snapped. 'It's time for another little funeral service.'

Cartney nodded, an evil grin on his face. 'And then?'

'Then,' Perov said quietly, 'We shall go and arrange a couple of surprises for Mr Steed. He should be feeling quite complacent again by now. The pressure has been off for over five hours. It's time we put it on again.'

CHAPTER 7

Steed checked his watch for the fourth time in half an hour. It was nearly eight-fifteen. A slightly worried frown creased his brow. Gambit and Purdey should have been back some time ago. At the very least, he would have expected one of them to telephone with a message. The thought triggered a sixth-sense response. Steed crossed to his telephone extension and lifted the receiver to his ear. A couple of abortive taps on the receiver rest confirmed his instinctive fear. The line was dead. It could be no accident.

He could wait no longer. Steed locked his study behind him, walked out to the hallway and put on his jacket and bowler. As a precaution, he rummaged through the umbrella stand, choosing his special brolly – the one with a spring-loaded stilleto built into the tip. Closing the front door tightly behind him, he strode briskly across the grounds to the large garage. He decidede to take the open Lancia. It was a warm night, and a breath of fresh air would do him nothing but good.

The car snapped smartly into life at the touch of the button, even though it had not been used for some time. Easing out of the garage, Steed nosed the Lancia round and purred down the drive at a pace which befitted the magnificent machine's looks of elegance combined with controlled power.

Steed always found that his choice of vehicle determined his driving style. In the Rover, he drove fast, accelerating abruptly and relying on the power brakes to bring him to sharp and sudden halts. In the Mini, he darted about erratically, yet with a sure, positive control on the steering column. In the Lancia, he always cruised.

It was just as well. Half way down the drive, passing between a short row of young ash trees, something glinted in the light of the evening sun.

Steed pulled the Lancia to a smooth stop and climbed out to investigate. Stretched across the drive, about three feet from the ground, was a thin but tough trip-wire. In another three or four feet the long bonnet of the Lancia would have hit it.

Steed regarded the wire for a few seconds, then returned to the car and backed it several yards up the drive. He rummaged in the boot, bringing out a large adjustable wrench.

Taking careful aim, Steed tossed the wrench towards the trip-wire. The heavy metal handle fell neatly on top of it, pulling it down three or four inches.

A loud explosion shattered the quiet peace of Steed's grounds. Across on the far side of the drive, one of the young trees sagged sideways then fell with a crash, its slim trunk blasted into a sappy, twisted mess of torn fibres.

Steed went to investigate, treading cautiously in case the booby-trap had a second string to its bow.

It had not. The crude ambush was a strictly one-shot affair. Or, more correctly, two-shot, since the trip-wire had been connected to the trigger mechanism of a double-barrelled shotgun, firmly secured by the base of a tree.

Steed looked at the shattered ash sadly. He had been rather looking forward to a neat, even avenue of shade in a few years to come. Now he would have to go to all the trouble of re-planting. It really was a nuisance.

The position of the blasted tree showed him how clumsy and inefficient the booby-trap device had been. Even if he had not seen the trip-wire, the shotgun had been lined up in such a way that its lethal load would have been discharged high above the bonnet of virtually any car, and several feet in front of the windscreen. A few stray pellets might, conceivably, have found their way into the front passenger section, but they could have done little damage.

The more Steed considered, the less he understood. The crudity of the device just didn't seem to fit in with the cold, calculated efficiency that his would-be exterminators had shown until now. If it were not stretching coincidence a little too far, Steed might easily have written off the booby-trap as a completely independent attack, nothing whatsoever to do with the earlier events of the day.

Still puzzled, he carefully checked the rest of the drive, removed the trip-wire and returned to the Lancia. Without further incident, he drove out to the open road and headed towards the Embassy for his meeting with Olga Perinkov.

Boris greeted him at the door with a guttural grunt of recognition. Steed noted, with some degree of satisfaction, that the man still walked very gingerly, his legs slightly apart. He led Steed along a series of featureless corridors to Olga's inner sanctum.

Olga greeted him with a warm smile on her face, but Steed did not have to look too closely to see the worried look underneath. Comrade Perinkov had troubles.

'Steed. Delightful to see you again so soon,' She gushed, stepping out from behind her desk with her hand extended.

Steed took her hand lightly, pressing his lips briefly across her knuckles. 'My dear Olga. You look as charming as ever,' he said, keeping up the air of friendly, careless banter.

'Vodka?' Olga produced a bottle and two conical glasses from a desk drawer.

Steed nodded, accepting one of the glasses and holding it out. Olga poured a healthy measure of Stolichnaya into it. Steed found it impossible to refrain from making a quick political dig. 'Ah, so apt a national spirit,' he murmured, holding the clear liquid up to the light. 'Crude, tasteless, yet deceptively strong.'

If the barb struck home, Olga betrayed no sign of it. She raised her glass. 'A toast, Steed?'

Steed tapped the rim of his glass against hers. 'To freedom?' he suggested, a wickedly sarcastic smile playing at the corners of his lips.

This time, Olga Perinkov's smile flashed off for just long enough to let Steed know he had touched a sensitive nerve. Then she regained her composure. 'To detente,' she said firmly.

Steed smiled. 'Ah yes . . . detente.' He followed Olga's lead in draining the glass at one gulp.

She gestured him to a large, plush couch. Steed sat down, appraising his hostess coolly as she spread herself decoratively beside him. Her arm curled lazily around the back of the couch, in what could have passed for a relaxed, almost nonchalant manner. Only the nervous twitching of the tiny muscles of her hand and wrist showed it was a ploy.

'Well, shall we get down to business?' Steed asked bluntly.

Olga raised one delicate eyebrow a fraction of an inch. 'Business, Steed?'

Steed smiled indulgently. 'Olga my dear. We have both been in this business long enough not to treat each other like simpletons. Shall we stop beating around the bush. You did not invite me here for a social chit-chat. Therefore, shall we get down to the first thing on the agenda?'

'All right Steed.' Olga's forced smile vanished at last. She straightened herself on the couch, crossing her hands on her lap. 'I'll stop playing games with you.'

'Especially card games, I trust?' Steed murmured softly.

Olga started, her eyes widening. 'How much do you know?'

Steed fished in his pocket, extracting one piece of the bisected King of Hearts. He tossed it down beside her. 'About half,' he answered. 'Which I suspect is about the same as you know.'

Olga nodded slowly. 'It was entirely Perov's idea,' she said quietly. 'He conceived a plan, worked on it for years, built it up . . . and finally put it into action as a dying act of defiance.'

'The House of Cards,' Steed murmured, under his breath.

Olga looked at him in surprise. 'You know more than I expected,' she said. 'Yes, that was the name of the operation. The House of Cards . . . the code name for a . . .'

'. . . A batch of sleepers,' Steed interrupted. 'Trained agents infiltrated into this country then put into cold storage until they were needed. I'd worked out that much myself.'

Olga nodded. 'I can add only a little more. Perov

dreamed up the plan over twenty years ago. He chose 13 agents, built a perfect copy of a typical English town back home. For five years the agents spoke English, acted English, studied everything about the English way of life. By the time they were brought over here, they were *English,* to all intents and purposes.'

'They were all conditioned to kill,' Steed put in. 'Brainwashed in some way. What method was used?'

'Each one of the chosen 13 was already a trained assassin,' Olga replied. 'They had killed many times before without compunction. As far as the conditioning is concerned, I am none too sure. Our methods have become so much more subtle in recent years. Then, I suspect the treatment was quite crude – almost Pavlovian. Simple habitual response, I should assume ... to pain, fear, possibly electrical stimulus of the hyperthalmus ... it existed, in a rather infantile stage at that time.'

'Crude perhaps ... but still chillingly effective,' Steed remarked, thinking of the cabbage-like Frederick. 'Cheated of their targets, these agents lapse into a catatonic state.'

Olga nodded. 'That would fit in with the thinking behind the operation,' she agreed. 'Each agent was given one specific task, a single target. Few of them knew each other's new identities, or new location in England. It all helped to make the scheme virtually imposible to break.'

'Exactly what was the purpose of the House of Cards?' Steed asked, flatly.

Olga spread her hands in an almost apologetic gesture. 'Now, it all seems so different,' she muttered. 'As you know, things have become so much more easy, even cordial, between our two countries. But then ...

the Cold War, the aftermath of Berlin . . . it was a difficult and dangerous time which seemed to call for dangerous measures.'

'The purpose, Olga,' Steed prodded, more firmly.

'Virtually to wipe out the security forces overnight.' Olga spoke in little more than a whisper. 'Had the occasion ever arisen, Perov could have activated each sleeper by his or her individual card. Within twenty-four hours, they would each have asassinated their individual victim. It would have been a coup d'etat, from which Britain might never have fully recovered.'

'But it was never used . . . why?'

'I told you . . . relationships became so much better between us. Double-agents sprang up, our security systems became more integrated, more information was pooled. We realized that we had far more to fear from the CIA than from your security forces. But the operation existed, and we could hardly dismantle it without raising some awkward questions. So we let it stay dormant, assuming that it would never be activated.'

'A case of letting sleeping dogs lie,' Steed suggested.

'Exactly. When Perov died, we should have been happy to let the House of Cards die with him. Unfortunately, he activated it, for some obscure personal reasons of his own.'

'Now you have something of a problem,' Steed said.

Olga Perinkov smiled thinly. 'You are so totally British, Steed. That incredible capacity for understatement. Yes, we have an embarrassing problem . . . but it is your people who are being killed.'

Steed shook his head. 'No,' he said firmly. 'Not yet, anyway?'

Olga stared at him in amazement. 'They have all failed?'

'Afraid so,' Steed answered, with mock concern.

Olga bristled. 'How many cards have been activated?'

Steed held up three fingers. 'A trio of hit-men so far . . . all misses.'

For a moment, Olga's lovely face became an angry scowl as a fierce, inner nationalistic pride surged up inside her. 'This decadent country,' she spat. 'It has made our people soft, flabby. They have become infected with the British way of life, like some insidious creeping disease.'

Steed grinned tauntingly. 'Strong words for a Cultural Attache, my dear Olga.'

She simmered down, collecting herself. 'I'm sorry, Steed. For a moment, you must have thought that I wanted this evil plan to succeed.'

'The thought did cross my mind,' Steeed admitted. 'But with the tase of vodka still in my mouth, and the toast to detente so recently from my lips, I dismissed it of course.'

Olga glared at him. 'Sometimes Steed I tend to forget your very strange British humour.'

'So do I, sometimes,' Steed murmured. 'Especially when people are shooting at me.'

The remaining anger drained from Olga's face. She looked at Steed with an expression of genuine concern . . . even, perhaps, a touch of fondness. 'Yes, I forget too just what danger faces you,' she said quietly. Reaching out, she grasped his hand in a friendly gestture. 'Although we are on opposite sides of the fence, I rather like you, John Steed. That's why I knew that I had to warn you. Your life is in terrible danger.'

Steed smiled unconcernedly, flipping up the halved King of Hearts with his fingernail. 'Not any more, it seems.'

Olga glanced down at the card, then up into Steed's

face again. She smiled sadly. 'Alas, Steed, you were always highly thought of . . . even thirteen years ago. Perov had great respect for you . . . so much respect that he allotted more than just one card to you. That much I *do* know.'

Steed accepted the back-handed compliment with a philosophical shrug. 'His faith in me is very touching,' he murmured. 'You wouldn't happen to know which cards, I suppose?'

'Only the very top of the pack, I should think. Perov was a stickler for protocol.'

Steed gave a short, grim laugh. 'So friend Perov still has an ace up his sleeve, so to speak.' He stood up, preparing to leave. 'I'd best start looking.'

'It will be like looking for your proverbial needle in the haystack,' Olga said hopelessly.

Steed laughed. 'Or the joker in the pack,' he countered. He moved towards the door.

Olga rose, running after him. She seized his arm, squeezing it. 'Take care, Steed.'

He nodded, seriously. 'Your concern is appreciated, my beautiful Olga. I find it quite flattering.' He stopped, turned, and looked her directly in the eyes. He bent forward quickly, planting a kiss full on Olga's moist, slightly parted lips. 'We really must get together some time, my dear Olga,' he murmured. 'Perhaps a cultural evening . . . at my place?'

Olga's face coloured up. She stepped back, trembling slightly. 'Perhaps,' she whispered, softly.

Steed smiled cheerily. 'I'll see myself out.' He turned the door handle, stepping out into the corridor to be greeted by the scowling Boris. Steed gave him an outrageous wink, swinging up his brolly and laying it across the bridged fingers of his left hand. He played an imaginary billiards shot in the air, noting with satisfaction that Boris actually winced at the memory, cupping his hands over his groin instinctively.

Outside, in the warm summer night, the light was just beginning to fade. Steed climbed into the Lancia, snapping on the side lights as he started the car up. He pulled away from the kerb causally, in the absence of any traffic coming up behind him.

A few yards in front, a yellow sports car screamed out of a line of parked vehicles, cutting across Steed's path and missing the long bonnet of the Lancia by inches. The sports car stopped abruptly, with a squeal of brakes.

Despite his gentlemanly good manners, Steed was sufficiently incensed to raise himself from his seat and glare over the windscreen. A few well-chosen words rose to his lips – most of them to do with the mental processes of the female gender in general, and their driving abilities in particular.

The female occupant of the yellow sports car opened her pretty mouth to apologize, the words dying on her lips as recognition dawned.

'John! John Steed!'

Steed's anger dissolved as he peered through the gloom and recognized the face behind the hauntingly familiar voice. A very beautiful face indeed, surmounted by a flaming corolla of red hair.

'Jo!' Steed could not repress the excitement in his tone, tinged with the faintest suggestion of disbelief. 'It's been so long.'

Joanna Harrington jumped over the side of the sports car impusively, not bothering to open the door. She ran towards Steed, her arms outspread and her lovely face glowing with happiness.

Steed responded with a fervour which seemed strangely out of character. His normal reserve vanished as he leaned over the side of the Lancia and swept the woman into a firm embrace. He held her tightly for several seconds, her cheek pressed against his. Finally, he pushed her away from him gently, his eyes searching her face with undisguised pleasure.

'It's good to see you again, John,' Joanna murmured, her voice slightly husky.

'And you.' Steed continued to admire her unashamedly. After a few moments, the shadow of a frown crossed his brow. His voice bore the merest hint of a rebuke when he spoke again. 'You went away . . . why?'

Joanna Harrington lowered her eyes. 'I had to,' she whispered sadly. 'It was the only way for me. We were close . . . far too close. It frightened me.'

Steed nodded gently with understanding as he remembered. Yes, it had been like that. Love – real love – had strong, strange powers. They could be frightening, especially when a woman was inexperienced in the ways of the world.

Fresh from a sheltered existence within convent walls, her life and its whole meaning shattered by a sudden and confusing loss of vocation, Joanna Harrington had ventured out into the harsh world of reality to find a new beginning . . . and had found John Steed instead. The depth of their rapidly-flowing relationship, and the sheer intensity of her own emotions must have put her under terrible strain.

Yet time was a great changer, and a great healer, Steed found himself daydreaming. It had been over four years. The past was gone . . . could there, perhaps, still be a future?

Joanna's next words shattered Steed's half-formed

thoughts abruptly. Her tone was one of unmistakeable apology. 'I got married, John. Two years ago.'

Steed's face was impassive. 'I hope you are happy,' he muttered evenly. 'You deserve happiness.'

Joanna shrugged. 'We get along,' she said quietly. 'Life is pleasant, untroubled. You could call that a form of happiness, I suppose. And you?'

Steed smiled distantly. 'Oh, I'm married,' he said, mysteriously. 'But then, I always was.'

Joanna's eyes flickered with the faintest expression of surprise, but she did not pursue the point. 'He's in the diplomatic service . . . my husband,' she went on. 'I'm an invaluable asset to him . . . a decoration, a committed, long-contract hostess.'

An awkward silence descended between them. Finally Steed spoke, a trifle hesitantly. 'Perhaps . . . perhaps we could have dinner one night?'

Joanna smiled wistfully. 'I'd like that John . . . very much. It will have to be in the next few days, though. I'm flying out to join my husband in Prague very soon.'

Steed had been half-expecting a polite refusal. He beamed with satisfaction. 'Tomorow night then?'

Joanna nodded. 'Tomorrow would be wonderful.'

'Where would you like to go?' Steed asked her. 'Anywhere you like.'

Joanna's eyes flashed with a saucy twinkle. 'There used to be a place I liked very much,' she murmured. 'A little place in the country. The ambience was beautiful and the maitre d'hotel was the most wonderful man in the world. Perhaps you remember it too, John? We had many happy times there.'

'And always a ride after dinner to aid the digestion,' Steed murmured, thinking of the many idyllic evenings they had spent together out at the stud farm. 'Yes, I remember it well.' He looked slightly apologetic. 'Alas, it is not quite what it was, I'm afraid. Business dropped off quite a lot . . . by a good fifty per cent, in fact.'

They laughed softly together, sharing the slightly sad joke.

'I think the maitre d'hotel is still the most wonderful man in the world,' Joanna said quietly. 'I'm sure he could still rise to a special occasion.'

Steed shsugged modestly. 'It will be spartan fare, I assure you. A less than lavish portion of Beluga caviar, a mere dozen or so fresh oysters, some strawberries and only a magnum of Dom Perignon to use as a mouthwash afterwards.'

'Perfect.' Joanna smiled happily. 'And the ride afterwards?'

'The ride afterwards,' Steed promised her. A fleeting look of doubt crossed his face. 'Are you sure, Joanna? Is it quite . . . diplomatic?'

She faced him squarely, her eyes flashing. 'You were always a perfect gentleman, John. You will not have changed. I trust you to observe the correct protocol.'

'Of course.' Steed nodded his head, briefly. He held out a hand. 'Until tomorrow, then?'

Joanna placed her hand inside his. 'Until tomorrow,' she confirmed, in a throaty whisper.

She turned away abruptly, walking back to her car without looking back. Snapping the powerful engine into life, she shot away from the kerb with only a brief wave of farewell over her shoulder.

Steed watched her disappear into the night. Long after she was gone from view, he sat quietly in the Lancia. There were many conflicting thoughts in his head . . . all of them loosely connected with a single, thin thread. Everything was welling up from the past . . . echoes and ghosts, faint shadows. It all had to mean something, Steed felt sure. But what?

Ghosts. Again, a single word fizzzled briefly upon the palate of Steed's consciousness, bursting like a champagne bubble and passing away before the full taste could be captured and savoured.

In a moment, it was gone. Still without the elusive answer he sought, Steed's mind returned to the present. With a small sigh, he reached to the car dashboard and brought the Lancia to life. He drove home at a fast pace, hoping that the cool wind of the rushing night air might clear some of the cobwebs from his mind.

CHAPTER 8

Cartney pulled the Citroen to a smooth halt at the rear of the crematorium. 'What now?'

Perov jerked a thumb casually over his shoulder at the two unconscious bodies slumped on the rear seat. 'Take them inside and put them somewhere nice and safe. We have work to do.'

Cartney nodded. 'I've got just the place. Then what?'

'Then get Doctor Tulliver round here as quickly as possible.'

Cartney's voice showed his surprise. 'Tulliver? What excuse shall I give him?'

Perov clicked his tongue against the roof of his mouth in a gesure of impatience. 'Use your brain, fool. He's a doctor, isn't he? Tell him there's an urgent matter of life or death to be attended to.'

Cartney showed his teeth in a stupid grin. 'Ain't that the truth?'

Perov waved his hand in annoyance. 'Must you use those decadent Western slang expressions in my presence? Just get on with it.'

Cartney shrugged the rebuke off lightly, muttering softly under his breath: 'When in Rome.' He climbed out of the car and opened the rear door. Pulling Purdey's limp form roughly from the back seat, he dragged it unceremoniously towards the back door of the crematorium.

Later, utilizing empty coffins for stools and a table, the two men sat in the dimly-lit store-room which adjoined the service chapel of the crematorium. A bottle of vodka gave them solace as they waited for the arrival of Tulliver.

A faint buzz sounded in the eerie stillness of the house of death. Cartney jumped to his feet. 'That will be Tulliver. Do you want to greet him?'

Perov shook his head. 'No, you go, Cartney. I think I shall give the good doctor a little surprise.'

As Cartney trotted obediently towards the door, Perov crept into a shadowy corner, concealing himself behind a stack of coffin panels propped up against the wall.

Tulliver sounded most put out as Cartney opened the door to admit him. 'This really is most irregular, you understand. Calling me at my private number at this hour of the night. I am not a general practitioner, you understand. I cannot even imagine how you came by my name.'

'You were most highly recommended, Doctor Tulliver,' Cartney murmured soothingly. 'Your name was specifically mentioned.'

'Very well. Take me to the patient,' Tulliver replied somewhat wearily.

Perov peered out from his hiding place as the two men walked into the room. Tullived glanced quickly around the gloomy store, a puzzled frown on his face.

'What is going on here? I see no-one. You said it was a most urgent matter . . . a dying man, you told me.'

Cartney giggled, nodding his head towards a few of the coffins. 'No dying men here, Doctor. Only dead ones.'

Tuliver stared at him. 'What nonsense is this? Are you insane, man?'

Perov's voice boomed out from the shadows. 'Insane,

Tulliver? What is insanity? You, of all men, should know the answer to that question.'

Tulliver started, his eyes darting around the storeroom seeking out the source of the hidden voice but seeing nothing. 'Who is that? Where are you?'

Perov spoke again, his voice taking on a gently mocking, chiding tone. 'Don't you recognize my voice, Tulliver? Don't you know me, the man who owns you?'

A touch of fear showed in Tulliver's jerky movements and the slight quaver in his voice. 'Owns me? What are you talking about? Am I in a place full of madmen?'

Perov stepped out quietly from the darkness, moving towards Tulliver. 'Oh yes, I own you, Doctor Tulliver. I always have done. You are mine, at my command, to obey my every whim.'

He stood a matter of inches from Tulliver's face, a mocking smile playing about his face. The doctor stiffened as recognition dawned upon him. His face went the colour of a fine cigar ash. His whole body trembled.

'Perov!'

Perov nodded slowly. 'Good, you do recognize me after all. For a moment, I feared that the passage of time might have robbed you of your old memories... and, perhaps, even of your old loyalties?'

Tulliver's lips trembled. 'Why have you brought me here?'

'You know why,' Perov muttered, quietly but firmly.

Tulliver shook his head violently. 'No, it cannot be ... it must not be. That was all in the past. I have a new life now, a dedication. I am a respected man... a humanitarian.'

'It *will* be,' Perov said chillingly. 'You belong to me, Tulliver . . . or should I use your real name, Ivan Skopovitch?'

Tulliver shivered at the use of the name he had discarded twenty years previously. 'Perov, you cannot mean to carry through your scheme. Not now, after so long . . . after so much has changed.'

Perov spread his hands in the air. 'What has changed, Ivan? The mother-country remains, our leaders may have been replaced, but the old ideology has not faltered. Your commitment can not have changed . . . can it?'

Perov finished on a threatening note. Skopovitch could hardly miss the point. 'Of course not,' he blurted out, falteringly. 'I am no traitor.'

Perov glanced down at one of the coffins. 'Good,' he murmured quietly. 'These things are no fit way for a man to travel the long journey to his homeland.'

'If I refuse to work for you?' Skopovitch questioned, already knowing the answer.

'You will not refuse,' Perov retorted flatly. You can not. You used the word "insanity" just now, Ivan. By definition . . . a human mind deranged, unable to function normally. Madness is a power, Ivan . . . a strong, strange power which takes over the human mind. There are other powers.'

As he spoke, Perov's hand dived into his pocket and emerged clutching a sheaf of halved playing cards. He fanned them out between his finger and thumb, the backs towards Skopovitch's face. Slowly, Perov's other hand strayed along the cards, finally selecting one and lifting it an inch or two higher than the others.

'It should not be necessary to use this,' Perov said softly. 'You should be with me of your own free will

. . . or did I train you too well, Ivan? Did I make you too English?'

Skopovitch's eyes were firmly fixed upon the back of the card. His entire body trembled violently. 'No,' he screamed. 'It will not be necessary, I promise you.'

'Good.' Perov slipped the cards into his pocket again. 'It is just as well. I want the full use of your brilliant brain, Ivan . . . not just the stupid robot implanted in it by your own devilish techniques.' He paused for a few seconds. 'I assume you have not forgotten your very special talents?'

There was a sad, wistful smile on his face as Skopovitch answered. 'No, I have not forgotten . . . even though I have tried, very hard.'

'Splendid.' Perov rubbed his hands together with glee. 'I have two clients for you, a man and a woman. I want them programmed as quickly as possible.'

'How quickly? Long-term conditioning takes time. Re-arranging a piece of equipment as complex as the human brain cannot be done in a matter of hours.'

Perov dismissed the objection with a careless wave of his hand. 'It need only be a temporary thing. I wish the subjects to perform one simple task, that is all. After that, they are both utterly expendable.'

'They will have to kill?' Skopovitch asked, miserably.

Perov nodded.

'Someone they already know?'

'A colleague . . . a friend, I suppose you could say. John Steed.'

Skopovitch looked dubious. 'You are asking a lot, Perov.'

Perov smiled broadly. 'I always ask for much,' he boasted. 'A man who demands only a little is a fool, a useless animal without ambition or vision. Besides, Ivan Skopovitch, I have faith in you.'

'I will need drugs . . . equipment,' Skopovitch muttered. 'They are at my laboratory.'

'I shall drive you there personally,' Perov responded immediately.

'A rare honour,' Skopovitch answered with undisguised sarcasm. 'I see that your faith in me is not matched by your trust.'

Perov thrust his arm around the man's shoulder, guiding him towards the door. 'Trust, my dear Ivan, is a luxury a prudent man learns to live without.'

Gambit returned slowly to consciousness through a long, black tunnel full of a thick, swirling fog. His head throbbed with pain, and bright pinpoints of light prickled behind his eyeballs. As his full senses returned, he realized that he was in total darkness.

He was also totally enclosed in a very small space. Flexing his fingers gently outwards, he encountered the smooth, hard surfaces of polished wood on either side of him. Reaching up, he touched a similar surface only a few inches above his chest. By stretching his body, he could make both the top of his head and the tips of his shoes tap hollowly against the walls of his cramped prison.

So he was in a box, or a crate of some kind! Gambit fought off a brief attack of claustrophobia and forced himself to remain calm. He lay still, breathing shallowly and pursuing logical paths of thought.

The air he was breathing was musty, but pure enough. Therefore, he was in no immediate danger of suffocation. Common sense told him that he must have been unconscious for some time, and the size of his prison would have contained only enough air for about half an hour of normal respiration. It followed, therefore, that some provision had been made to allow a certain amount of fresh air into the box.

He rapped gently on the sides of the box with his knuckles, listening carefully to the sound. From it, he deduced that the wood was less than an inch thick. Bearing in mind the size and shape of the container, it could not be terribly strong. Escape was therefore not only possible, it was relatively easy . . . especially for a man who could snap a four-inch block of pine with a single blow of his hand. With these comforting thoughts, Gambit relaxed to consider his next move.

Escape was easy . . . but would it be practical? What lay outside the box? Was he being guarded? All these questions flashed through Gambit's mind in a matter of seconds, and he realized that he had no way of knowing the answers. He lay quietly for a long time, straining his ears for the slightest sound which might give him some clues to work upon. There was nothing. Wherever he was, Gambit mused, it was as silent as the grave.

This thought brought a sudden, chilling revelation as to the exact nature of his wooden prison. The gently tapering shape of it should have given him the clue earlier.

He was shut up inside a coffin! Gambit shuddered involuntarily. A crate was one thing, but a coffin was most definitely another! It had decidedly unpleasant overtones.

Gambit's immediate decision was based upon ancient, irrational fears rather than upon cool logic. It was time to perform a passable imitation of the late Harry Houdini! Gambit lay back, emptying his mind of everything before beginning to draw in the power of total concentration which enabled every muscle and sinew to perform like tempered steel.

No matter what lay in wait outside, Gambit was breaking out. He tensed his body slowly as the power built up, inexorably. Mind over matter: perhaps even a cage of solid steel could not contain him now.

In a single, convulsive explosion of mental and physical energy, Gambit let rip. His knees came up against the top of the coffin with the force of steam-hammers, whilst his arms flailed out sideways and his body stretched out from toes to the back of his head. Every part of his body found a contact against solid wood . . . and continued outward as though they encountered no resistance. With a tearing, splintering crash of rending wood, the panels of the coffin burst asunder. The enclosing structure fell apart around him. Gambit was free.

He jumped to his feet, standing rock-still. His keen ears probed the darkness, searching out the slightest sound. Only when he was completely satisfied that he was alone in the darkened room did he reach into his pocket and draw out a cigarette lighter. With a press of his thumb, the piezo crystals clashed together, releasing their intrinsic energy in a spark of static electricity. The tiny gas jet leapt into flame.

The small, flickering light served only to direct him to the nearest light switch. Gambit's finger hovered on it as lightly as a butterfly as he strained his ears once more. Still, there was no sound. He snapped on the light, blinking as the sudden illumination blinded him.

It was several seconds before he was able to see enough to take in his surroundings. He stood in the service chapel of the crematorium, completely alone except for another coffin laying a few feet away from the shattered remains of his own.

'Purdey!' The word formed silently on his lips. Walking on his tiptoe, Gambit crossed to the coffin and knelt beside it. He tapped very gently on one side with his knuckles 'Purdey?'

There was no reply. Bending his head, Gambit placed his ear flat against the wooden top and listened. Very faintly, he heard the distinctive, regular sound of shallow breathing.

Gambit's heart surged with relief. He tapped again, a little more insistently. 'Purdey, wake up.'

There was a faint rustle of movement from inside the coffin, followed by several louder knocks as Purdey awoke in panic and struck out against the enclosing walls.

Her voice came to him, thick and slurred. 'Wherrami?'

Gambit placed his lips close to the coffin lid and whispered. 'Purdey, you're all right. Relax. It's me, Mike. I'm going to get you out of there right now. Just don't panic, lie still.'

He glanced around for a suitable instrument to prise open the lid of the coffin. Like his own private tomb, the lid had only been loosely tacked down to allow a free passage of air. It would be child's play to open it without a sound.

Gambit's eyes fell upon a claw hammer laying discarded in one corner of the chapel. He placed his lips against the coffin once again. 'I'm just going to get something, Purdey. Be back in two or three seconds.'

He rose to his feet, crossing the chapel silently and picking up the hammer. Returning, he slipped the forked claw between the lid and the side of Purdey's prison and levered gently. The lid rose a fraction of a centimetre with a faint squealing of nails in wood. In a matter of moments, it was done. The coffin-lid was loose enough to pull off by hand.

'Shut your eyes tight,' Gambit hissed, giving Purdey a couple of seconds to comply before slipping his fingertips under the coffin-lid. He wrenched it off, standing it quietly against the nearest wall and returning to look down at his companion's prone, still body.

Gambit felt a surge of awe, gazing at her lovely face and her lush body. It was a feeling he had experienced many times before, and he never quite got used to it. A mischievous smile spread across his face. 'My God, you'd make a beautiful vampire,' he murmured quietly.

Purdey's eyelids flickered a couple of times, then cracked open. She took in her surroundings quickly and calmly, showing no sign of being fazed. Looking up at Gambit, she gave him a wry smile. 'Looks like we've blundered our way into the dead centre of things.'

Gambit smiled, reaching down to take her outstretched hand and help her to her feet. 'Welcome back to the land of the living.'

Purdey grinned briefly before a worried frown crossed her face. At once, the cheerful badinage was finished. 'Which brings us to the million-dollar question . . . why?' she murmured thoughtfully. 'Why are we still alive?'

Gambit considered the question seriously for a moment. Finally, he shrugged. 'A good point,' he mused. 'And one to which I have no quick and easy answer. I can only suppose they . . . whoever *they* are . . . want us for some specific reason.'

Purdey nodded. 'Right! Are you planning to stick around to find out what it is?'

'No way,' Gambit said, firmly. 'You feel up to making a move?'

Purdey nodded. 'I suppose the obvious thing is to

try the front door first.' She walked quickly up the aisle between the two tiers of seats in the service chapel and tested the heavy oak doors. They were firmly locked. She returned to Gambit, a rueful smile on her face. 'A little *too* obvious, perhaps?'

Gambit's eyes fell upon the other, small door which led into the adjoining store-room. He nodded his head towards it. 'Next logical choice,' he observed.

Side by side, they approached the door cautiously. Gambit's fingers closed around the handle, twisting experimentally. There was no movement.

Gambit glanced at his companion apologetically. 'So much for the logical approach,' he muttered. 'Shall we try a little brute force and ignorance?'

Purdey shrugged her assent, stepping back to give him room. Gambit moved back a couple of feet, twisted his body sideways and brought up his right leg. With a flying kick, his heel connected with the door a few inches below the lock, smashing it clear out of the surrounding wood frame.

Gambit turned to Purdey, grinning triumphantly. With an exaggerated gesture, he bowed, sweeping his hand through the open portal. 'After you, madame.'

'Thank you, kind sir.' Purdey tripped lightly through the doorway into the store-room.

. . . To come face to face with a glowering Cartney, Luger in hand. He looked decidedly upset.

'You woke me up,' Cartney complained, bitterly. 'I don't like being disturbed.' The gun in his hand trembled menacingly.

'Terribly sorry,' Gambit muttered with mock concern. 'Look, why don't you just lie down again and resume your little nap, and we'll just sneak out nice and quietly.'

The joke was not appreciated. Cartney stepped forward, swinging the heavy gun towards the side of Gambit's head.

Gambit's reactions were lightning-fast. He ducked, weaving to one side. The vicious blow cleaved harmlessly through the air above him, twisting Cartney on the balls of his feet and throwing him off balance. Gambit made the most of his temporary advantage. His right hand shot out, bunched knuckles connecting hard against Cartney's moving wrist. The stunning blow served its purpose well. Cartney's fingers snapped open as every nerve in his hand was abruptly numbed. The Luger flew into the air, disappearing into a corner with a dull clatter.

Snarling with pain and rage, Cartney lashed out angrily with his foot, catching Gambit a painful blow just under the knee. Limping slightly, he fell back a few paces as Cartney bent over and began a running head-butt aimed at Gambit's belly.

He moved sideways – but not quite quickly enough. Cartney's shoulder crunched into the extreme right of his hip, spinning him round and throwing him back through the door into the service chapel. He fell badly, catching his side against the side of the coffin which had recently housed Purdey. Gasping painfully, Gambit only just managed to drag himself to a crouch as Cartney closed in on him again, kicking out at the side of his head.

Gambit weaved sideways again, feeling the rush of wind as Cartney's heavy boot whistled past his ear. Gambit shook his head, trying to clear it. The effects of the gas had still not quite worn off. His reactions were still dulled, slowed down dangerously. Under normal circumstances, Gambit could have handled a clumsy fighter like Cartney with no trouble at all. In his present condition, he was in real trouble.

Struggling to his feet, Gambit prepared himself for Cartney's next attack. The man moved slower now, with greater confidence. Instead of rushing in, counting on weight and speed, he realized that he had the upper hand, and thus had more time to consider and plan his moves. He circled his prey warily, feinting a couple of attacks to drive Gambit in the direction he wanted.

Not quite realizing that Cartney had started to plan a strategy, Gambit backed away from the threatened openings. Too late, he realized that his befuddled mind had been tricked, led into a trap. As he backed, his heel caught against a raised projection, almost tripping him. Glancing down quickly, he saw that he had backed all the way to the three small steps which led up to the tiny pulpit.

Cartney, sensing that his opponent would be at a severe disadvantage confined in a small space, made the most of his opportunity to charge forward. Gambit had no choice but to back up the steps into the pulpit itself. Trapped inside it, he prepared to tackle Cartney at close range.

The big man bounded up the steps in pursuit of his trapped quarry, his arms outstretched. His huge hands reached out and grasped Gambit around the neck, his thumbs pressed neatly into place against the man's windpipe. Using the full weight of his body, Cartney pressed Gambit back over the edge of the pulpit, threatening to snap his spine like a dry twig.

Gambit's arms flailed uselessly at his sides as he tried to find enough room to swing in a double punch to the heavy man's kidneys. His hands banged ineffectually against the wooden sides of the pulpit, then against something else.

Gambit's fingers explored a small control panel, flicking over buttons and switches. He groped blindly, seeking something loose which might conceivably be used as a weapon. There was nothing.

One of the switches moved under the pressure of his fingers. With a sudden, faint hum of power, an electric motor snapped into life.

The sudden sound snapped Cartney's concentration for just a moment. He glanced out over Gambit's shoulder towards the source of it. Gambit, his head swimming for lack of oxygen, felt the pressure on his windpipe lessen fractionally. It was all he needed. Summoning the last ounce of energy in his body, he straightened up, reached down with both arms and cupped his hands under Cartney's groin. With a mighty heave, he lifted the heavy man clear of the wooden base of the pulpit and heaved him into the air.

Cartney's body sailed over his head, clearing the rim of the pulpit by a good six inches. Headfirst, he plummetted downwards, landing heavily on the low pedestal which served to display the coffin during the brief cremation service.

Gambit staggered backwards, half-falling down the steps as he tried to get to his opponent while he was still stunned. Half way there, Gambit realized that he wasn't going to make it. His legs turned to jelly beneath him and he crumpled forwards on to his face. Through misted eyes, he looked up and saw that Cartney was moving again . . . but not of his own volition!

Gambit's fiddling with the control panel had activated the conveyor belt which transported the coffins through the black curtains into the incinerator. Now

Cartney's senseless body was moving along the conveyor belt slowly but surely.

Gambit struggled to get to his feet, but it was useless. He screamed to Purdey. 'Switch the damned thing off, for God's sake. The control panel is in the pulpit.'

Purdey reacted quickly, sprinting over to the pulpit and running up the steps. Panicking, she punched buttons and threw switches at random.

The silence of the crematorium was suddenly shattered by the loud, unnerving sound of music. The sonerous, morbid notes of the Death March echoed out from the concealed loudspeakers.

Purdey flicked two other switches hopefully. The black curtains swished back silently on nylon runners as Cartney's head disappeared through the small opening. The music ceased abruptly, to be replaced by a soft choral rendering of the Requiem Mass. Other than that, there was no change in the automatic process Gambit had inadvertently initiated. Cartney's booted feet disappeared into the dark, rectanguar hole at the end of the conveyor belt.

There was a sudden, dull roar as the gas jets ignited automatically, rising to a hissing crescendo. Above the sound, a brief, bloodcurdling scream was ripped from Cartney's throat . . . then there was a terrible silence.

Gambit pushed himself to his feet groggily and stared morosely into Purdey's apologetic face. 'Very nice. Very tastefully done,' he muttered sarcastically. 'Did anyone tell you before that you might have missed your vocation?'

Purdey pulled a face and jerked her head towards the drawn black curtains. 'Looks like things are hotting up,' she observed, with black humour.

'Yeah,' Gambit breathed, shrugging off the unfortunate setback philosophically. He had been hoping to persuade Cartney to answer a few of the questions which had been plaguing them. Now they were as much in the dark as they had been all along. It was a bitter disappointment.

'Well, that seems to wrap things up around here,' Purdey murmured, after a last glance around the crematorium. 'Shall we make a move?'

'Yeah. Let's get out of here,' Gambit grunted, turning towards the store-room.

'I think not.'

Perov stood framed in the outer doorway, a small Mauser pistol in his hand. Behind him stood Tulliver-Skopovitch, his arms laden with equipment.

Perov jerked the pistol fractionally. 'Back against that wall,' he commanded.

Gambit stared at the man in open astonishment, recognizing him immediately. 'Perov!'

The man smiled. 'Ah, you recognize me, Mister Gambit. How flattering. Yes, as you observe I am remarkably fit and agile for a corpse. Not a trace of rigor mortis about my person.' He stepped in through the doorway, glancing around with mild surprise. 'Where is Cartney?'

Gambit flashed him a defiant grin. 'He had to go . . . rather suddenly.'

'Go?'

'Yes. He was sorry he missed you,' Gambit shot back. 'Really burned up about it, in fact.'

'Enough!' Perov barked nastily, waving the gun again. 'You are an enterprising man, Mister Gambit. You did well in disposing of Cartney. He was a strong man. That is a good omen. You will doubtless be even more efficient in exterminating John Steed for me.'

Gambit's lips curled in a sneer. 'You've got to be crazy, Perov.'

Perov ignored the insult. He shook his head calmly. 'No, not at all,' he murmured conversationally. 'They do say that true genius borders on insanity, I must admit. Fortunately, I have always remained firmly on the right side of the dividing line.'

'You're very modest,' Purdey put in sarcastically.

'A realist,' Perov corrected. 'I have never seen the point of non-productive human emotions. They tend to impair one's judgement, get in the way of important decisions.' He regarded Gambit piercingly. 'I meant exactly what I said, Mister Gambit. In a few hours, you – or your companion – will leave this place and kill John Steed for me. It will depend upon which one of you gets to him first.'

He turned to his waiting companion. 'Do come in, Doctor Tulliver,' he invited, reverting to Skopovitch's cover name. 'Allow me to introduce you to your patients.'

Tulliver looked at Purdey, his lips quivering. 'You didn't tell me one of them was a woman,' he muttered miserably. 'You can't make me do it . . . it's inhuman.'

'I *can* make you do it,' Perov snapped testily. 'Please don't forget that, Doctor.'

'Do what?' Purdey asked, calmly.

'Oh, I'm sure Doctor Tulliver will explain it all to you as he goes along,' Perov retorted carelessly. 'He's probably more up on the technical terms than I am. He probably has a dozen long words to describe his craft. As a simple layman in these matters, just like yourselves, I lump them all under the embracing general term in popular usage.'

'And that is?' Purdey wanted to know.

'Brainwashing, my dear.' Perov's teeth showed in an evil leer. 'Not that I am suggesting your brain is at all dirty, you understand. I'm sure you have a very clean brain indeed.'

Perov indulged himself in a laugh at his own sick joke. Purdey regarded him with undisguised loathing. 'Mike's right. You're crazy.'

Perov's laughter ceased abruptly. A momentary look of rage crossed his face, but he controlled it. He turned to Tulliver. 'Enough time has been wasted, Doctor. Get on with what you have to do.'

Meekly, Tulliver opened his black bag, drawing out a hypodermic syringe and a rubber-capped phial of pale yellow fluid. Upending the phial, he loaded the syringe carefully, squeezing the plunger and squirting a few drops of the substance into the air. Satisfied, he moved towards Purdey, reaching out to grasp her arm.

His touch was gentle. 'This won't hurt you, my dear,' he cooed softly. 'It's just a drug to relax you, make you docile. You'll find it makes your muscles feel very weak, however. That's the only physical effect, I promise you.'

Despite her fear, Purdey smiled bravely. 'Great bed-side manner you've got there, Doc.'

'Don't worry,' Tulliver murmured soothingly, as he slid the needle into the crook of her elbow.

'Oh, I'm not worrying,' Purdey quipped back. 'I'm sure life as a zombie is quite enjoyable, once you get used to it.'

Her eyes glazed over as the drug took quick effect. Tulliver supported her as her legs buckled beneath her. Gently, he lowered her to the floor and re-filled the hypodermic, glancing at Gambit. 'A slightly bigger dose for you, I think,' he went on, keeping up the out-of-place professional manner.

Perov watched the operation with satisfaction. When he was satisfied that both Purdy and Gambit were sedated, he put the Mauser away in his pocket. 'I will leave you to get on with it then, Tulliver,' he snapped. 'Now I must go and co-opt some help. It really is a nuisance. Cartney was most helpful to me.' He moved towards the door. 'Is everything under control, Tulliver?'

Tulliver looked down at the slumped bodies of the two Avengers. He nodded. 'Everything is under control.'

'Good.' Perov gave the doctor a strange, meaningful smile. 'I know you won't let me down.'

Opening the door, he stepped out into the night.

CHAPTER 9

Gambit felt light-headed, even slightly amused. The drug had a certain hallucinogenic effect, heightening sensation and creating a mental feeling of well-being. The fact that he could hardly move a single muscle in his body didn't really seem to matter. If anything, it was a rather pleasant, relaxing experience.

He chatted happily as Tulliver set up his equipment. The drug did not appear to affect his sight, hearing or speech. Gambit was fully aware of everything going on around him, and anxious to discuss it in a bantering, light-hearted manner.

'What are you doing now?' he enquired cheerily as Tulliver connected wired electrodes to the backs of his hands and each side of his temple.

'Connecting you up to an electro-encephalagraph,' Tulliver informed him. 'It monitors your brainwaves.'

Gambit accepted this information calmly. 'Then what?'

Tulliver finished wiring up the ECG machine and turned his attention to a slide projector. 'Some pieces of film,' he muttered, over his shoulder.

Gambit giggled like an excited child. 'Oh good. A movie show,' he said happily. 'Got any Popeye films? I used to like Popeye films.'

Tulliver turned to regard his patient, a sad smile on his face. 'It's not that sort of a picture show,' he murmured. 'I am about to find out what your secret inner fear is.'

'Fear?'

'Everybody has one,' Tulliver said in a low voice. 'Fear of heights, enclosed spaces, drowning, darkness ... there are a thousand spectres lurking in the depths of the human subconscious. Find the individuals's specific phobia and you find his weakness. Play upon that weakness and you have the means to destroy his mind.'

Gambit still nodded happily. In his drugged state he quite liked the doctor. He was a good man ... a friend. Someone to be trusted, helped. He felt a strong urge to assist the good doctor in every way possible. He wanted a fear ... therefore Gambit would give him one.

'And the film clips ... they will help you find my fear?' he asked.

Tulliver nodded. 'Most of the standards are here,' he answered. 'The electro-encephalagraph will record your mental reactions to several dozen different things. It will not take long.'

He switched on the projector. Gambit sat back in his chair, his eyes glued to the small screen. It began to flicker with rapidly-changing images. Shots of precipitous cliffs, underwater films, hordes of rats, small dark rooms, insects crawling over human bodies, enlarged views of a spider eating its mate, a raging fire.

Gambit felt a vague unease as the images flashed in front of his eyes. He felt a sense of guilt as time progressed and he failed to react. Somehow he sensed that he was letting the good doctor down. Tulliver wanted him to react to one of the images, and Gambit had so far failed to do so. He gathered his confused mind together, concentrated on the desire to help.

Tulliver snapped the projector off abruptly. 'Snakes,' he muttered flatly. 'You hate snakes.'

Gambit felt relieved. The good doctor seemed happy

and satisfied. That was good. It meant that Gambit's attempt to please him had succeeded. He had taken a single image completely at random . . . that of a diamond-back rattlesnake poised to strike . . . and effected the sort of reaction he supposed his friend would expect of him. The ploy had obviously succeeded extremely well, for Tulliver now busied himself setting up the next stage in the conditioning process.

The doctor erected a four-sided screen all around his subject, carefully lining up special projectors at strategic points. From an extensive portable library of films and tape cassettes, he selected those best suited to his purpose and made everything ready. Finally, he slipped a pair of earphones over Gambit's head, switched everything on and stood back, his face drawn with sadness. Tulliver did not like what he was doing. The years had given him a vocation to cure the human mind, not destroy it.

He took a last look at Gambit before turning away and removing himself from the scene, abandoning a pitiable creature in the dark world of his own subconscious fears.

Gambit sat, unmoving, as the process consumed all of his available concentration. On all sides, three-dimensional holographs turned his immediate environment into a pit of writhing snakes of every description. His ears were filled with the hissing, slithering sounds of reptiles – every sensation heightened by the effects of the drug coursing through his veins. A vague, distant recess of his mind registered the fact that Tulliver had walked away, and Gambit relaxed full at last, his last minor worry swept aside. It was better that his friend the doctor leave him alone, for if he had stayed, he might have been disappointed. Gambit had felt a vague sense of guilt at having tricked the good doctor – albeit for the most benevolent of motives. Gambit had always rather liked snakes, and all reptiles in general. He found them rather fascinating, their sensuous movements quite soothing.

Now, there was nothing to worry about. Gambit sat back and prepared to enjoy himself. It was all like a pleasant dream, a fantasy. The only discordant, mentally jarring note was the hissed name which came over the earphones at regular intervals, always coinciding with a visual image of a deadly snake, its fangs exposed and dripping with poison.

'Sssteed. John Sssteed.'

The name somehow failed to fit in with the rest of the dream, so Gambit's drugged mind struggled to reject it. John Steed was his friend too, as well as Doctor Tulliver. The snakes were friendly, soft and soothing.

The insistent repetition of Steed's name began to irritate, jangle sensitive nerves in the depths of Gambit's brain. He struggled to rationalize, fit it in with the other images which buffeted his subconscious.

Snakes were gentle creatures, for the most part. They rarely attacked without being provoked.

The thought popped, unbidden, into Gambit's head, and he seized upon it eagerly. It was a good mental image to have, for it could be slotted into the fabric of the fantasy. If John Steed had to be a snake-like character, then it must be so. Just like a snake, Steed only became deadly when threatened, in danger. Like a snake, Steed was strong, sinewy, quiet to move and well able to wriggle out of trouble.

Contented again, his mind untroubled, Gambit relaxed once more in the company of all his dear friends – human and reptilian. The hours slipped by like fleeting moments, for the drug wiped away all concept of time. The film and sound tape looped time and time again, but Gambit failed to register the recurrence of specific images.

The dream ceased abruptly. Gambit returned to a state of semi-consciousness on a screaming express train, hurtling out of a long dark tunnel towards the daylight. His body felt charged up like a dynamo. His muscles surged with pent-up power, his mind strained against a leash which was almost severed.

The blinding wall of light dancing in front of his eyes slowly dimmed into a roundish, dull blur, finally resolving itself into the features of a human face. A slow, stupid smile crept across Gambit's own expressionless features as he recognized Doctor Tulliver – although he was not quite sure why the sight should afford him so much pleasure.

'How do you feel, Mister Gambit?' Tulliver asked him gently. 'You should be feeling well, happy... better than you have ever felt before.'

Gambit nodded as the suggestion took root in his mind. 'Yes, I feel on top of the world,' he agreed.

'Good.' Tulliver nodded to himself, then glanced across to Perov, who waited just out of Gambit's immediate range of vision. 'He's all yours.'

Perov crossed the room quickly, staring deep into Gambit's glazed eyes.

'Do you recognize me, Mister Gambit?'

Gambit nodded. 'Nikolai Perov.'

'Fine,' Perov said, beaming. 'Now, Gambit. You have a very important task to perform. Do you remember what it is?'

Gambit struggled to remember. There *was* something important in the back of his mind . . . something which he had been about to do, before the dream, before time had stopped. An image of a boa constrictor flashed across the surface of his consciousness, without any reason. The snake reminded him of a name. John Steed.

He remembered. He had been trying to get to Steed . . . to warn him, tell him of Joanna Harrington's possible connection with the House of Cards. Trying to get to Steed . . . before the telephone box . . . the gas . . . the strange, haunting dreams about snakes.

Gambit's eyes brightened. He nodded happily as memory returned. 'I must get to Steed,' he murmured. 'It is very important . . . I must get to John Steed.'

Perov chuckled gloatingly. 'Excellent, excellent.' He beamed at Doctor Tulliver. 'You have done a wonderful job, doctor. I congratulate you.' He turned his attention back to Gambit. 'You must go now. Go and fulfil your mission.'

He ushered Gambit to the rear door and watched him go on his way. Walking back into the store-room, he confronted Tulliver once again. 'Now we will see to the girl. Go and fetch her.'

Tulliver's lower lip trembled. 'She's already gone,' he blurted out. 'I sent her on her way a few minutes ago . . . just before I woke Gambit.'

Perov's face clouded with anger. 'You had no right,' he blazed. 'I gave you no such order. I wished to check her conditioning, just like Gambit.'

Tulliver hastened to calm down the raging Perov, reassuring him. 'She was perfectly conditioned, I promise you. I wished only to save you time and trouble, Comrade Perov.'

He stood, trembling. Perov's eyes regarded him

piercingly. It was impossible to overlook the man's obvious unease. 'You're lying, Tulliver,' Perov hissed at last. 'You are lying to me . . . aren't you?'

Tulliver shook his head violently. 'No, I swear it, Comrade. I did just as you asked.'

His pleas ended in a scream of pain as Perov lashed out, striking him across the face. 'The truth, Tulliver. I want the truth.'

Tulliver broke down. 'All right, I did not condition the woman. I merely kept her drugged, then let her go a few minutes ago as I told you. I could not do what you asked to such a beautiful young woman, Comrade. I conditioned the man Gambit exactly as your orders . . . surely the girl does not matter.'

'Everything matters,' Perov blazed. 'That is why my plans always work . . . because I leave no room for mistakes . . . or for fools.'

His hand dived into his jacket pocket, coming out holding the Mauser. Tulliver stared at the gun in horror.

'No, Perov . . . you cannot.'

'I will not tolerate disobedience,' Perov hissed in a quiet, yet menacing voice. 'And I cannot forgive broken loyalty.'

He squeezed gently on the trigger, twice in succession. Tulliver screamed, briefly as the first slug ripped into his chest, flinging him backwards. The second bullet caught him under the heart as he fell. Tulliver was dead before he hit the floor, collapsing half in and half out of the empty coffin which had imprisoned Purdey many hours before.

Perov looked down at his body dispassionately, slowly slipping the gun back into his pocket. He reached out gingerly with one foot, prodding Tulliver's limp form until it lay, full-length, in the coffin. Kicking the dead man's elbows, he placed his arms across his chest and smiled to himself.

'Poor fool,' he murmured under his breath. 'You were always so predictable, Ivan Skopovitch. You did exactly what I expected you to do. I thank you for that, at least.'

Turning away from the dead man, Perov extracted the sheaf of halved playing cards from his inside pocket and shuffled quickly through them, drawing out the eight of hearts. With a final gesture, he ripped the halved card into small pieces, then carelessly threw them over his shoulder. The tiny shower of torn pasteboard fluttered down like confetti over Tulliver's body.

CHAPTER 10

Steed was worried. Twenty-four hours had passed, with no word from Gambit and Purdey. His telephone was dead. He had not forgotten the booby-trap rigged up in his driveway. All in all, it was not a very reassuring picture.

He soothed his ruffled nerves with a healthy measure of brandy, forcing himself to look upon the bright side. He knew and trusted his companions well enough to know that they could handle themselves under most circumstances, and it was not unusual for them to be out of contact for quite lengthy periods. It was highly probable that they were following up some lead provided by Suzy Milner.

The matter of the telephone was even easier to rationalize. His stud farm was in open countryside, miles from anywhere. All power and telephone cables had to travel many miles across fields and open countryside. Failures were common enough, under such circumstances. They could go unreported for days on end.

This optimistic view was not really fully credible to a mind so attuned to potential trouble as John Steed's but he made it do. There were, after all, other things to be considered.

He finished off his brandy and set about preparing for his dinner date with Joanna Harrington. It was a task to which he set himself fully. Earlier, Gambit had fantasized his colleague as a snake-like creature: Now, if he could have seen Steed smoothing the sofa cushions and placing the bucket of iced champagne just within reach of a reclining figure, he might well have seen him more as a spider, preparing its web to entice a most delectable fly.

There were two distinct and separate aspects to a worthwhile life, Steed often philosophied. Business . . . and pleasure. Steed was a firm believer in devoting one's full attention to both, at the correct and proper time. Accordingly, he carried on putting that philosophy into actual practice.

He dipped one finger tentatively into the ice-bucket, then glanced at his watch. It seemed perfectly in order. The Dom Perignon could well afford to drop a couple of degrees, but Joanna was not quite due to arrive. By the time she did, the champagne should be just about perfect.

Steed nodded to himself with satisfaction, turning his attention to the dinner table. He picked up the silver cutlery in a clean white napkin, giving it a last quick polish. Re-arranging the position of the slim, jet-black candles, he lit them with something of a flourish, crossed the room and turned out the main light. It was perfect. Romantic without being sloppy, impressive without ostentation.

Satisfied with the arrangements, Steed retired to his favourite chair and sat down to relax and await his guest.

The doorbell chimed softly. Steed rose, crossing towards the door. The last, fleeting worries about Gambit and Purdey evaporated from his mind. Joanna Harrington left no room in his thoughts for anyone else.

Steed threw open the front door and extended a hand to assist her over the threshold. His eyes sparkled as he took in her total appearance. She looked absolutely stunning! Joanna had obviously dressed and prepared for the evening with the utmost care. Steed felt a warm glow inside at the equally obvious inference that the date was as important to her as he felt it was to himself.

'You look absolutely ravishing,' he told her, with no overtones of false flattery. It was a mere statement of fact, an intelligent and honest observation.

Joanna accepted it modestly, merely smiling to express her pleasure in giving pleasure. 'I'm not late, am I?'

Steed smiled. 'Perfectly on time,' he assured her. He glanced again at his watch, looking up and smiling. 'The champagne should be ready in thirty-five seconds exactly.'

Joanna chuckled. 'Knowing you, John, you're probably not joking.'

Steed faked a shocked look as he escorted her into the dining room. 'Joking, Jo? Surely you know that I would never joke about a thing as serious as champagne?'

He slipped an arm gently around her waist as they walked through into the dining room, showing her to the plush sofa. Joanna settled herself down gracefully, looking up at him with a gentle smile before casting her eyes around the rest of the room. 'Little has changed,' she observed.

Steed smiled wistfully. 'I'm not a man who cares too much for change, Jo.' If the words carried the faintest hint of rebuke, Joanna chose not to notice.

Steed bent down and pulled the magnum of Dom Perignon out of the ice bucket with a faint, shimmering rattle. Grasping it with the precision of an expert, he wrapped a clean serviette around the neck and deftly peeled off the foil and wire. The cork started to rise smoothly as the wire came free. With a loud pop, it flew up, bounced off the ceiling and rolled across the carpeted floor. Joanna rose from the sofa with a little squeal of excitement, scooping it up. She held it in the air. 'May I keep it, John? A little souvenir . . . of tonight?'

Steed regarded her with a sad smile. 'A going-away present?' he murmured. Joanna made no answer, popping the champagne cork into her handbag.

Steed took two slim tulip glasses from the cocktail cabinet and poured the champagne. He carried them across to the sofa, handing one to Joanna before sitting beside her. He raised his glass in the air. 'A toast?'

'To the past?' Joanna queried.

'To everything,' Steed muttered firmly. He pressed his glass against hers, rolling the thin stem between his finger and thumb. The bowls of the tulip glasses caressed each other silently. It was a curious erotic image.

They fell silent for a while, sipping and savouring the champagne. Steed refilled the glasses and sat back in the sofa. 'We can eat whenever you are ready,' he murmured. 'It's only a cold meal, I'm afraid. Oysters, some caviar, turkey pâté, some sliced pheasant and cold capon and a caesar salad.'

Joanna shivered deliciously. 'It sounds wonderful.'

Steed shrugged. 'I'm not much of a housekeeper, I'm afraid.' He rose, crossed to the stereo unit and slipped a Debussy LP on to the turntable. Adjusting the volume to a comfortable background level, he returned to the sofa.

Joanna had picked up a small silver-framed photograph from the occasional table. She studied it with a certain feminine jealousy, taking in the clear, perfectly-moulded features of Tara King.

'Beautiful,' she murmured, the tone of her voice inviting a reply from Steed.

He nodded emphatically. 'She was a magnificent filly,' he agreed. 'We had some fine sport together. The only trouble was, she got a little too high-spirited ... it's the Irish blood, you know. In the end, she got to liking her oats too much and I had to sell her to an Arab prince. I believe he shot her in the end, poor thing.'

Joanna looked – and sounded – shocked. 'Shot her?'

Steed leaned in towards her, his eyes falling on the face of the photograph for the first time. His face flushed suddenly, with unaccustomed embarrassment. He coughed awkwardly, temporarily lost for words. Reaching out, he picked up another identically-framed snapshot and handed it to her, just managing a faint, shame-faced smile. 'Sorry, I thought you were talking about Connemara Princess.'

Joanna studied the second photograph of a magnificent Palamino mare, slowly understanding the mistake. She grinned broadly.

'It's that cleaning lady of mine ... always moving things about,' Steed added, relieved that Joanna displayed such a flexible sense of humour.

To ease his embarrassment, Joanna stretched out a slim finger and gently caressed Steed's cheek. 'Oh John, you really are a most remarkable man,' she murmured throatily.

'With a penchant for remarkable women,' Steed retorted, flashing her a seductive smile.

Again, Joanna accepted the implied compliment gracefully. She replaced the picture of Connemara Princess, nodding briefly at the portrait of Tara King which she still held. 'And beautiful ones, it seems. She was a friend?'

Steed nodded. 'A good friend.'

Joanna chuckled mischievously. 'A very good friend, perhaps?'

'A very good friend,' Steed confirmed.

Joanna allowed the faintest suggestion of jealousy into her eyes. 'A very, *very* good friend?'

Steed saw a trap, and skated neatly around it. 'A gentleman may admit to one "very",' he said, smiling. 'But two "verys" and he is no longer a gentleman.' He took the portrait gently from her fingers and replaced it, face-down, upon the table. 'Let me get you another glass of champagne.'

Joanna jumped to her feet. 'No, let me . . . please. I want to pamper you.'

Steed settled back comfortably in the sofa. 'I really don't deserve such treatment,' he demurred, a little half-heartedly.

'Nonsense.' Joanna bent over to the ice-bucket and lifted the magnum of champagne, filling both glasses to their brims. She turned back a little too quickly, the heel of her shoe catching in the thick pile of the carpet and tripping her. She lurched slightly forwards, the glasses jumping in her hands. One of them slopped awkwardly, spilling champagne over its brim and on to the long sleeve of her evening dress. Joanna looked down at the wet mark irritably. 'Oh dear, clumsy me.'

Steed jumped to his feet at once. 'Let me get you a clean napkin to wipe it down,' he suggested.

Joanna smiled gratefully. 'Oh, would you, John? Thank you very much indeed.'

'It's nothing.' Steed crossed to the dining table. As his back was turned, Joanna's hand dived to her handbag, fumbling quickly inside it. By the time Steed turned back towards her, napkin in hand, she was studiously gazing at her wet sleeve once again.

Steed dabbed at it with the napkin gently. 'There, that should do it,' he murmured finally. 'It shouldn't stain. Champagne is a most forgiving beverage, in more ways than one.'

He sat down again, bending to pick up the two glasses of champagne from the carpet. Joanna moved suddenly, pressing herself against his side and throwing her arms around him. 'Hold me for a few moments, John,' she pleaded.

Steed straightened, gazing into her eyes. Joanna opened her arms in an inviting embrace. 'Just hold me tight,' she repeated.

Steed responded to the invitation eagerly. Moving along the sofa, he snuggled up close to her side and let her wrap her arms around him once again. He slipped his own hands around her slim waist. Their eyes met, fusing together into a silent courtship ritual. There was a brooding, pregnant silence.

Moments passed. Joanna's head pressed forward, gently, slowly. Steed, hypnotised by her overpowering presence, sat rigid, staring raptly into her face, feasting on her beauty. The distance between their two pairs of lips dwindled to fractions of a centimetre. Joanna's mouth glistened moistly, her lips parting in an invitation to a kiss.

The sudden blast of a gunshot, quickly followed by the shattering of glass disturbed the romantic silence. Steed, his senses as keen as ever, threw a protective arm around Joanna Barrington's neck, dragging her down behind the protection of the back of the sofa. Almost in one smooth movement, he rolled on to the floor, sprang to a crouch and sprinted across the room towards the dining room table. He upended it, plunging down behind it for cover. The cutlery, fine china and cold buffet crashed to the carpet in a mess.

Outside, a foot kicked open the glass door of the french windows leading out into the grounds. A lithe figure jumped through, into the room, keen eyes taking everything in at once.

Steed, peering around the overturned table, let out a curt expletive as he recognized the intruder. He rose, slowly, his face a strange mixture of puzzlement and anger.

'Do you usually made such a dramatic entrance?' he demanded, his voice a couple of octaves higher than normal.

Purdey stood, legs braced apart and both hands curled around the butt of a small, pastel-coloured automatic. 'Steed. Don't move,' she snapped, urgently.

Steed took a step towards her.

'I mean it, Steed,' Purdey warned. 'Freeze – right where you are.'

Shaking his head in bewilderment, Steed did as he was bid. Purdey jumped across the room, coming around the back of the sofa. She trained the automatic on the cowering figure of Joanna Harrington. 'All right ... sit up, slowly, with your hands above your head.'

Joanna trembled with fear. She pulled herself up to a sitting position, staring towards Steed with fear-filled eyes. 'John ... who is this woman? Is she mad?'

Steed's eyes widened expressively. 'I'm certainly beginning to think so.' He whirled on Purdey. 'Well, just what is going on?'

Purdey's gun never wavered from Joanna for a second. 'Pick up her handbag, Steed,' she muttered, in a cold voice.

He hesitated. 'Purdey, I refuse to do such a thing until you tell me what on earth you are playing at.'

Purdey's voice rose to a scream. 'Damn you ... do

it, Steed. There may not be much time. Pick up her handbag.'

Shrugging hopelessly, Steed crossed the floor and picked up the handbag from the floor.

'Open it,' Purdey snapped.

Steed shook his head. 'Purdey, if you think I am going to open up a lady's handbag, you are sadly mistaken,' he murmured. 'What has come over you?'

Purdey forced herself to stay calm. Her voice took on a new edge . . . cool but menacing. 'Please Steed – just do exactly what I say. I know you are a gentleman . . . but I want you to open that bag and tip the contents out on to the table.'

The sheer urgency in her voice overrode Steed's natural objections. He unclasped the bag, carrying it across to the occasional table and upending it. With a faint clatter, a variety of objects fell out. A lipstick, a small compact, a bunch of keys, some loose coins and a gold cigarette lighter.

. . . And half of the Ace of Hearts!

Steed gazed down at the accusing card, utterly dumbfounded. His lips trembled. 'No, it can't be,' he muttered, in a shaken voice. His eyes darted to meet Joanna's, bearing a silent plea. 'Tell me it isn't true, Jo.'

She stared at him sullenly, her beautiful face devoid of any emotion.

Steed looked down at the contents of the handbag once again. He looked quickly up at Purdey, and for a second, there was a hopeful light in his eyes and a faint note of triumph in his voice. 'There's no gun, Purdey. No weapon at all. She came to warn me.' He turned again to Joanna Harrington. 'Isn't that right, Jo? You came to warn me – not to kill me. Just like David Milner.'

Purdey was thrown for a fraction of a second. She had expected a gun. 'Then she planned something else,' she snapped, with certainty. She tossed the gun across to Steed who caught it expertly. 'Watch her, Steed.'

Reluctantly, Steed turned the automatic on the silent Joanna. Purdey glanced around the room, questioningly. Her eyes fell upon the two glasses of champagne. With a sudden bound, she jumped upon them, picking them up from the carpet and carrying them over to the small table. Upending them both, she tipped the contents on to the napkin which Steed had used to wipe down Joanna's dress. The champagne ran through and the last few bubbles fizzled into extinction.

'There,' Purdey shouted, triumphantly, pointing accusingly at the soaked serviette.

Steed stared at it, his heart sinking. On top of the white napkin, a gelatin capsule rested, not quite dissolved. Inside it was a clear, colourless liquid, which in a few moments more would have been absorbed into Steed's drink.

'Poison,' he muttered, badly shaken. He glanced, sadly, at Joanna. 'How could you Jo? I thought we meant something to each other.'

She looked equally miserable. 'We did, John. I had no choice, no choice at all. They promised me it would be quick, utterly painless. I could not have borne to see you suffer.'

Steed shook his head. 'Oh, Jo,' he murmured, bitterly. He gestured over to Purdey, handing her back her gun. 'Take her away Purdey. Lock her up somewhere.' He turned his eyes away.

'No.' Joanna screamed, jumping to her feet and clinging on his arm. 'Let me go, John . . . I swear you'll never hear of me again. The idea of prison . . . I'd die, John, I know I would.'

Fighting the lump in his throat which threatened to choke him, Steed shrugged off her desperate clutch and moved a few paces away from her. He spoke over his shoulder, still unable to look her in the face. 'You asked me if I ever married, Jo,' he muttered, distantly. 'Well, I *did* marry – just once. I married a job, a profession. I took solemn vows to defend this country and bring her enemies to justice. I have been a very faithful husband.'

He crossed to the cocktail cabinet and poured himself a very large brandy. Purdey waved the gun at Joanna Harrington. 'You heard what the man said. Let's go.' She turned towards the door, pushing Joanna ahead of her.

'Drop the gun, Purdey.'

She started to turn, jolted by the sudden shock of Gambit's voice.

'Move another inch and you're dead. I mean it.' Gambit screamed at the top of his voice.

Purdey froze, still holding tightly on to the gun.

Gambit's voice was choked with conflicting emotions. 'God damn it, Purdey, I mean what I say. Please drop that gun.'

Purdey held herself rigid. She spoke calmly and spoke slowly, without turning around. 'You're bluffing, Mike. You haven't got a gun.'

'Don't try to call it, Purdey. God only knows I'd hate to kill you, but I will if I must.'

She began to pivot, very slowly on her heels. Gradually, she turned to face Mike Gambit, who stood framed in the open french windows. There was a relieved look on her face as she saw his empty hands. 'I thought you were bluffing, Mike.'

Steed had watched the bizarre performance with absolute astonishment. Now he spoke for the first time since Gambit's sudden appearance. 'Now I know you're mad, Purdey. You too, Mike.'

Purdey cast him a sideways glance. 'Mike came here to kill you, Steed. He's not himself . . . he's been brain-washed . . . conditioned to hate you.'

Gambit smiled wryly. 'Oh no, Steed. It's the opposite way around. It's Purdey who intends to kill you. She's the one who has been brainwashed.'

'Don't take any notice of him Steed,' Purdey hissed. 'Don't trust anything he says. He doesn't know what he's doing . . . his mind has been tampered with.'

Steed threw down the remainder of the brandy in his glass and stared at the two deadlocked figures dumbly. He was quite convinced he was having some kind of a crazy dream. 'Would someone please have the decency to make some sense?' he pleaded. 'Some-one just give me the faintest inkling of what is going on?'

The two antagonists ignored him. Their eyes were firmly fixed upon each other, sharing a mutual distrust. Gambit moved, placing one foot tentatively forward. The gun jerked in Purdey's hand.

'Stay right where you are Mike. I'll shoot, I promise you.'

Gambit shook his head slowly. 'Now *you're* bluffing, Purdey. You couldn't shoot me down in cold blood. I'm your friend, Mike Gambit . . . remember. You had a bad dream . . . it's all right now. I'm here to help you.' He took another step forward.

Purdey's body trembled. 'Don't try to treat me like a silly little schoolgirl, Mike. You know I will use this gun if I have to.'

Gambit's hand came up, his fingers outstretched. 'Give me the gun, Purdy,' he murmured in a soothing voice. 'Just give me the gun and everything is going to be all right.' He made one more forward step, so that his fingertips almost brushed the muzzle of the automatic. 'The gun, Purdey,' he prodded gently.

Purdey's finger tightened on the trigger. Every nerve-ending in her body told her that Gambit was about to make a move, lunge towards her. The trigger eased back, the small amount of slack taken up. She fought to control the tremors which rippled through her body. At any second, she would plant a .32 calibre bullet deep into Mike's brain. It was a horrible thought.

Mike Gambit moved, in a blur of speed. Purdey screamed, horror flooding her brain as she squeezed the trigger. The crash of the shot echoed around the room.

Gambit felt the heat of the slug as it passed by, a matter of half an inch from the side of his head. His thrusting fingers had got to the gun's barrel in the very nick of time, pushing it just far enough aside before Purdey's reflexes had made her fire. She had no chance of a second shot. Gambit muttered just one word: 'Sorry,' and punched her full in the face. She fell as thought pole-axed, the gun tumbling harmlesly from her nervous fingers.

Whilst the strange performance had been going on, Joanna Harrington had been inching around the room, towards the french windows. Now, as the gun tumbled to the floor, she saw her chance, and took it. She made a run for the open grounds, kicking off her shoes as she fled.

Gambit dived to the floor, scooping up the automatic. He ran to the window, taking aim on her fleeing figure, plainly silhouetted in the pale moonlight. 'Steed?'

'No,' Steed snapped. 'Let her go.'

Gambit turned, a little puzzled, as Joanna disappeared into the shadows at the end of the driveway. Although he said nothing, his raised eyebrows posed the question.

Steed shrugged sadly. 'Where she comes from, the price of failure is death,' he muttered. 'We are not giving her freedom . . . or her life.'

'I shouldn't be too sure of that,' Gambit retorted. 'Perov's still alive.'

He had expected a shocked reaction from Steed, but all he got was a thoughtful grunt. 'You don't seem surprised,' he said.

Steed smiled knowingly. 'He always was a cunning old fox,' he said, with a tinge of admiration in his voice. 'As I said before, the absolute master of the double-play. This is definitely his style.' He became serious again, glancing down at the unconscious Purdey. 'Now, will you tell me what you two have been up to?'

Gambit gave him a concise run-down on the events since leaving the Milner cottage. Steed listened intently, occasionally nodding and giving sparse breath to a pensive murmur. When Gambit had finished, Steed again looked down at Purdey, who was beginning to moan under her breath. 'Well, I suppose we ought to do something about poor Purdey.'

Purdey snapped back into full consciousness, aware of a pain all up the left side of her face and something cold, wet and rather sticky over her left eye. She reached up, poking at the offensive object before grasping it between finger and thumb. She pulled it away and held it in front of her nose, regarding the rather sorry-looking lamb chop with distaste.

'Sorry, old girl, it was the best I could do. The freezer was right out of beefsteak,' Steed said apologetically. He knelt beside her, his fingers probing her face very gently. 'It doesn't look as though it is going to bruise,' he comforted her. 'Mike must have pulled his punch, as it was you.'

Purdey stroked the side of her face ruefully. 'It certainly doesn't feel like it,' she complained, thinking of Mike Gambit and remembering, she leapt to her feet with a start. 'Where is he? Did he get away?' she demanded.

'I'm here, Purdey.' Mike's voice spoke gently from behind her.

She whirled in alarm, but seeing his friendly, smiling face, she relaxed. 'Mike . . . are you all right?'

'Fine,' he assured her. 'And you?'

Purdey nodded. 'Tulliver couldn't go through with it,' she said quietly. 'It was just too much for him to brainwash a woman after all these years. I figured he had conditioned you, though.'

Gambit laughed. 'He tried,' he told her. 'I guess I'm just too thick for brainwashing to work on me.'

They laughed for a few more seconds, before the same thought struck them both simultaneously. Their smiles faded abruptly, to be replaced by a look of shocked realization.

'My God, I nearly killed you,' they both chorused in unison.

The moment of tension lasted for several moments, finally passing away. Both Gambit and Purdey found relief in nervous laughter, giggling helplessly for several minutes.

Steed regarded them morosely, finding it impossible to join in their high spirits. The thought of Joanna weighed heavily upon his mind. Eventually, his brooding silence seemed to emanate out in a positive wave which engulfed his companions. Their laughter subsided, and they were serious again.

'I guess we all had a close call,' Gambit observed, flatly. 'We need to be a lot more on our toes. We could be running out of chances.'

'There is a good side to it, however,' Purdey put in. 'Friend Perov is also running out . . . of sleepers.'

Steed nodded thoughtfully. 'Milner, Spence, Frederick, Cartney . . . Jo,' he murmured quietly. 'Five down, and seven to go. That's still better than two to one. Not the best of odds, even in a two-horse race.'

'You're making a basic assumption which has already proved wrong,' Gambit corrected him.

Steed raised one eyebrow quizzically. 'And that is?'

'That every one of the thirteen sleepers is still alive, still available and still susceptible to conditioning,' Gambit said. 'Look at the facts so far and that patently is not true.'

'Expound,' Steed said, simply.

'You just mentioned five names,' Gambit told him. 'You did not count Tulliver, so that makes six. Out of that six, both Milner and Tulliver refused to carry out their allotted tasks. That makes a thirty-three per cent failure rate so far. I'm willing to bet that at least one more of the sleepers has either died, or managed to set up a new life completely under cover some time in the last thirteen years. Looking at things that way, it leaves Perov with only three, or maybe four, agents still at his disposal. Slightly better odds, wouldn't you agree?'

Steed nodded thoughtfully, impressed by Gambit's reasoning. 'You could be right,' he admitted.

Purdey suddenly had a thought of her own. 'It might not even be a two-horse race,' she blurted out. 'Perov may not have accounted for a last minute entry . . . an outsider.'

Both Steed and Gambit stared at her in amazement. Purdey was not usually given to profound statements.

She saw their slightly sceptical looks and shrugged them off. 'Maybe we are all forgetting Olga's role in this,' she went on. 'It seems to me that she has just as much incentive as we have to stop Perov. The Commissariat isn't going to be too pleased when they find out she has made a lash-up of her newly-acquired control. Her head is on the block as well.'

Steed thought of his earlier conversation with Olga Perinkov. Purdey's assessment of the situation seemed sound enough. There was still one basic flaw, however. Perov had obviously activated the House of Cards for a specific reason. Revenge was too petty a motive, it did not fit in with the man's character. That he should have unleashed such a deadly force merely to topple Olga from her new seat of power was equally preposterous. Therefore, her role in the affair had to be a subservient one . . . a mere coincidence, or an inescapable by-product. The only key to the whole mystery seemed to lay in isolating and identifying Perov's real reason for faking death and activating his sleepers. That key had to be found . . . and quickly.

Steed glanced at his wristwatch. It was nearly midnight. A good time to consider sleeping on the problem. He turned to his companions. 'I don't know about you two, but I think I've had just about as much as I can cope with for one day. I suggest we all get a good night's sleep and apply fresh minds to the problem first thing in the morning. You had both better stay here . . . and sleep with a gun under your pillows.'

'Good idea,' Purdey said, brightly. 'If you can't beat them . . . join them.'

Steed and Gambit looked at her oddly.

'Pardon?' Steed murmured.

Purdy grinned. 'Sleepers,' she said, cheekily.

Nobody laughed at the joke.

CHAPTER 11

Purdy awoke first, and in a rare maternal gesture, fixed breakfast for them all. The three Avengers sat around Steed's dining table eating fresh Charenton melon, eggs Benedictine and Melba toast – all washed down with freshly-percolated black coffee.

Gambit dabbed at the corners of his mouth with a fresh serviette. 'You'd make me a wonderful wife some day,' he murmured appreciatively.

Purdey smiled, keeping up the long-running joke which they had shared ever since they first came together. 'I couldn't stand the strain,' she told him. 'You're in a high-risk occupation.'

Steed, mediator and father-figure as always, presided over their friendly banter with a slightly jaundiced eye. 'Talking of occupations,' he muttered, bringing them back to earth with a gentle bump.

Gambit and Purdey gave him their undivided attention. 'Sorry, Steed,' they both muttered.

Steed drained his coffee cup. 'To business, then?'

Gambit nodded. 'To business.'

Steed pushed his plate aside and cleared a small space on the tablecloth. Selecting the salt and pepper shakers, three sugar lumps and a selection of tea-spoons, he set up an impromptu battle plan in front of them. He placed the three sugar lumps in a line. 'Here we are, then,' he started.

'Sweet,' Purdey muttered, under her breath. Steed gave her a fleeting glance of disdain.

'We assume that we are the target, for some reason,'

Steed went on, arranging the salt and pepper shakers opposite them. 'And this is Perov, with at least one bodyguard or heavy constantly by his side.' He scattered the spoons at odd intervals around the perimeter of the table. 'These, we will assume, are the remainder of the sleepers, still under cover and not yet activated.' He glanced at both his companions in turn. 'Fair enough?'

Purdey nodded. 'So to get at us, Perov has to get to one or more of them first?' She gestured to the teaspoons.

'Right,' Steed agreed. 'Which means he is going to have to make a move . . . away from us, primarily.' He slid the pepper and salt across the table, leaving the thre sugar lumps unguarded. 'Now what?'

Purdey reached out, scooped up the three lumps of sugar and popped them into her empty cup. She poured fresh coffee on top, picked up a spare spoon and stirred vigorously. 'We disappear,' she said brightly. 'Go into hiding.'

Steed groaned with exasperation. 'Really?'

Gambit couldn't help seeing the funny side of it. He grinned broadly. 'I hope you realize you've just drowned all of us?' he pointed out to Purdey.

She sipped at her coffee before replying. 'Again, you've forgotten my missing piece . . . Olga,' she said, putting down her cup. She picked up the sugar bowl and placed it immediately behind the salt and pepper.

Steed looked at her blankly. 'Are you trying to tell us something?' he enquired in a slightly sarcastic voice.

Purdey nodded. 'Simply that Olga Perinkov must have a much better idea of where to look for Perov than we have,' she explained. 'She must know his haunts, his hiding places, and his possible contacts. Therefore, she is in a much better position to keep tabs on him than we are. So we watch her . . . and she should lead us to Perov?'

'Why should she?' Gambit asked, not quite following Purdey's reasoning.

She gave him a pitying glance. 'As I said last night . . . because her head is on the block,' she explained. 'If she can't clear up this mess, she is as dead as Perov is supposed to be. They'll ship her back in a crate before you can say Uncle Joe Stalin.'

Steed stared at her, dumbfounded. Suddenly, the light of realization dawned in his eyes. He thumped the table with his clenched fist. 'Of course,' he blurted out. 'You've put your pretty little finger right on it.'

Purdey's beautful eyes opened wide in astonishment. 'I have?'

'Of course,' Steed said excitedly. 'That's the key to Perov's motivation. That's what we couldn't figure out . . . why he should have gone to all this trouble. His head was on the block, too. That's why he faked his own death. Why he activated his sleepers.'

Gambit shook his head dumbly. 'Not quite with you, Steed.'

'Look, Perov was up for the chop . . . right?' Steed said, more calmly.

'Right,' Gambit agreed.

'So all he had to look forward to was a trip home in a crate, or a job digging salt in Siberia. It was time for desperate measures . . . and the House of Cards is about as desperate as you can possibly get.'

'I still can't see why wiping us out was going to help him much,' Gambit said, still puzzled. 'The Commissariat aren't exactly known for holding the scales of justice. You can't think that Perov hoped to balance his failure by proving that his out-of-date scheme still worked.'

Steed shook his head. 'No – that's exactly where all our thinking has been wrong,' he said. We made the automatic assumption that Perov deliberately activated his sleepers to carry out their original tasks. I think it was a wrong assumption.'

'Then why?' Purdey wanted to know.

'Think back,' Steed urged. 'Why is Perov's neck on the block in the first place?'

'He failed to deliver the goods,' Purdey said.

'Exactly. The goods in question being Professor Vasil. Important enough goods to mean all the difference between life and death to Perov.'

Gambit suddenly understood. 'You mean we aren't the prime target after all?'

Steed nodded. 'That's exactly what I mean. Another wrong assumption. We have assumed that Perov activated the House of Cards out of pique, or some misguided attempt at revenge. I don't think he did. I believe that this whole business has been a highly elaborate smokescreen – to confuse and cover up the main issue. We are not the target . . . we are just in the way of the target. The real target is Vasil himself. Getting to him is the only way on earth that Perov can save his skin.'

'But that's impossible,' Purdey put in. 'There's no way that Perov can get to Professor Vasil.'

Steed looked dubious. 'That's what I would have thought,' he murmured. 'Until recently, I would have thought a lot of things were impossible. Right now, I'm not so sure about anything any more.'

Steed jumped to his feet. Purdey looked up at him. 'Where are you going?'

Steed dressed hurriedly. 'There's just one thing I *am* sure of,' he called over his shoulder. 'Professor

Vasil is a mighty important store . . . and I ought to be minding it.'

Gambit also jumped to his feet. 'Want us to come along?'

Steed waved him down. 'No. As long as you don't know where Vasil is, you can't tell about it. I have to do this on my own.'

'Well what do you want us to do? Just sit around here and wait?' Purdey asked.

Steed strode towards the door. 'If you want to make yourselves useful, you could try putting the squeeze on the lovely Olga . . . perhaps find out if she knows where Perov might have gone to ground.'

He walked out without another word. Gambit and Purdey faced each other across the dining table, both slightly bemused by the rapid turn of events. They heard Steed start up the Rover and ease it out of the garage. He cruised slowly down the driveway, the memory of the crude booby-trap device still fresh in his mind.

He reached the end of the drive safely, and nosed the Rover out into the road. Thrusting down the clutch pedal, he gave a couple of quick taps on the accelerator, goading the 3½ litre engine into roaring life, clearing out the carburettors. Steed's attention was firmly fixed ahead of him, his eyes looking right and left for passing traffic before setting out on to the road. Had he glanced in his rear-view mirror, he might just have caught a glimpse of Nikolai Perov, emerging from behind the cover of a thick rhododendron bush.

Perov looked at the back of the car and drew back his right hand. With a careful underhand lob, he tossed a small metal object on to the car's rear bumper. It fell with a faint click, locking itself securely into position with its magnetic base. Satisfied that the radio transmitter and homing device was safely in position, Perov ducked down behind the bush again until Steed had found a gap in the passing traffic and roared off down the road. Only when the noise of the engine had faded into the distance did he stand up and rub his hands gleefully together.

'Perfect. Absolutely perfect. Just as I planned,' he muttered to himself in a jubilant whisper. He raised one hand in the air, giving a pre-arranged signal. From the depths of the undergrowth, three more figures rose into view.

Perov addressed them in turn. 'Bassnet, Clements . . . you stay here and take care of Gambit and Purdey. You need not kill them unless you have to.' He turned to the third man. 'Come along, Bates . . . let us get to the helicopter.'

Back in the house, Purdey paced the dining room moodily. There was something niggling at the back of her mind which she could not quite identify. There had been something wrong in Steed's flow of logic – her female intuition told her so. But what was it?

She passed the occasional table. Glancing down, she saw the glistening poison capsule, left where she had tipped it out on to the serviette. She bent to pick it up, rolling it between her finger and thumb carefully. She glanced over to Gambit. 'You know, there's something fishy about this,' she said, holding the capsule up in the air.

Gambit shook his head. 'Doubt it. It's more likely to be strychnine . . . or cyanide,' he observed.

'Idiot!' Purdey dug a long red fingernail into the

soft gelatin of the capsule. A clear liquid bubbled out on to her fingers. She raised them to her nose, sniffing carefully. Then, slowly, she lowered the punctured capsule to her mouth.

'Purdey!' Gambit's voice screamed out in fear as he saw her pop the poison capsule into her mouth.

She clamped her teeth down on it, feeling the liquid contents squirt against the roof of her mouth.

'Oh my God.' Gambit rushed to her side, trying to force open her jaws.

Purdey pushed him away brusquely. 'What are you doing, Mike?'

He gazed at her with horror-filled eyes. 'You've gone crazy, Purdey. The tension has got to you. You're too young to die . . . too beautiful.'

Purdey preened. 'Do you really think so?'

Gambit waved his arms wildly in sheer exasperation. 'Look, let me get you to a doctor. There might still be time.'

Purdey moved away from him, pacing the room once again. 'You see, there's been one thing bothering me all along,' she mused out loud. 'And that is Perov's consistent failure to kill any of us. When Milner came to warn Steed, for instance. Perov picked him off with a telescopic rifle. He could easily have shot Steed at the same time. He didn't. Why?'

'I don't know, Purdey. Now please will you let me get you to a doctor?' Gambit pleaded with her.

'And again when Perov booby-trapped the drive,' Purdey went on. 'He could have killed Steed then . . . but he didn't. The device was deliberately made to fire above the car . . . almost like a warning signal.' She paused, opening her mouth and pointing down her throat. 'And now this. Joanna could have brought a gun, a knife, even a grenade with her. She had plenty of time to dispose of Steed in a dozen different ways ... yet she failed.'

Gambit's eyes rolled hopelessly. He expected Purdey to fall, writhing in agony, at any second. 'What are you trying to say?'

'That this has all been a fake,' Purdey said, triumphantly. 'Perov has fooled us all along the line. Remember what Steed said about him ... what a cunning old fox he was?'

Gambit nodded. 'The master of the double-play,' he murmured.

'Except that this is a triple-play,' Purdey muttered. 'This time, he really excelled himself. Perov never wanted Steed dead ... he wanted him scared, scared for Professor Vasil's safety. So scared, that he would go to check up on Vasil's hiding place ... just as he has done now. Don't you see, Mike? We've played right into Perov's hands. Steed is leading him to Professor Vasil at this very moment. We have to get after him, Mike.'

Gambit looked panic-stricken. 'But we can't, Purdey. There's no time. We have to get you to a doctor ... you're poisoned, you're dying.'

Purdey regarded him as though he was an imbecile. 'Do I look as though I'm dying?' she demanded.

Gambit looked at her. 'Well, no,' he admitted. 'But the capsule ...'

'Another fake. A bluff,' Purdey said. 'It was filled with water.'

Gambit's face glowed with relief. 'So you're not dying?'

Purdey groaned. 'You can be remarkably slow on the uptake at times, Mike Gambit.'

A fluttering, mechanical sound suddenly came to

their ears. Purdey rushed to the window, gazing out across the open countryside surrounding the stud farm. Less than half a mile away, a small helicopter rose slowly above a line of trees, hovered for a while and then set off in a westerly direction.

Purdey reacted at once, again obeying blind instinct. She rushed to Mike's side, clutching at his sleeve. 'Come on, we've got to get going quickly,' she urged.

'Where?' Gambit wanted to know. 'Which way?'

It was then that Purdey gave birth to the immortal line which finally laid a million gangster-film clichés in their grave.

'Follow that helicopter,' she screamed.

CHAPTER 12

Purdy led the way to the front door. Flinging it open, she prepared to sprint towards the garage.

Three gunshots cracked out. A few feet in front of the porch step, three small showers of gravel from the drive spewed into the air. Purdey ducked back through the door in double-quick time, slamming it closed.

'Trouble?' Gambit asked.

'Trouble,' Purdey confirmed. 'Friend Perov doesn't leave much to chance, does he? We have what I believe is known in the trade as a rear-guard action to take care of. They're out in the grounds somewhere.'

'How many?' Gambit wanted to know.

Purdey shrugged. 'I didn't hang about to count them. Two, maybe three.'

Gambit paused to think for a couple of seconds. 'We need a little firepower,' he decided quietly. He rushed back down the passageway into Steed's private armoury. When he came out again, he was adjusting the strap of a Sterling sub-machine gun around his shoulder. He grinned at Purdey, patting the short stock of the gun. 'This should even things up a bit.'

He moved into position by the front door, drawing in a deep breath. 'Ready?' he asked Purdey.

She nodded silently.

'OK. Go out through that door at a run . . . and keep running,' Gambit told her. 'Don't stop until you're safely in the garage. I'll cover you.'

Purdey inched the door open, looked back at him

and crossed her fingers. Gambit gave her a reassuring wink. 'You'll be all right, girl.'

'Tell me that in ten minutes time,' Purdey shot back at him. She tensed herself, threw the door open wide and bounded down the porch steps in a crouching, weaving sprint.

Gambit stepped out on to the top step and swung the Sterling round in a wide arc, spraying the grounds with lead. There was no return of fire. His finger locked on the trigger, Gambit kept up the hail of bullets until the gun was empty. He glanced sideways just for long enough to see that Purdey had made it to the safety of the garage before throwing himself back into the house to change the magazine. A dozen automatic slugs chewed into the woodwork around the frame of the door either side of him.

Gambit clicked the new magazine into position and fired off a half-dozen shots into the air to test it out. He waited, crouched behind the door-jamb until he heard the sound of the Lancia's engine roaring into life. He screamed briefly at the top of his voice before throwing himself out through the door again. 'Go, Purdey.'

Gambit ran sideways towards the garage, still fanning the Sterling with his finger jammed down on the trigger. A couple of loose shots slammed into the walls of the house behind him, but the two gunmen were not brave, or foolish enough, to take time and aim properly. The screaming hail of bullets from the Sterling were pouring out at random – but they were covering a lot of ground.

Gambit was less than half-way to the garage when the Lancia screamed out with a squeal of rubber and a rattle of flying gravel. Purdey, crouched low over the wheel, could only hope that she was travelling roughly in the right direction. The car bounded over two of Steed's prized azalia beds, demolished a row of sweet peas and ploughed across the croquet lawn, leaving a deep, twin line of tyre tracks across the flawless surface.

Gambit sprinted obliquely towards the oncoming car. With a flying leap, he landed on the old-fashioned running board and continued firing over the top of Purdey's bent head, hanging on to the side of the bucking car with his elbows.

Regaining the drive after flattening three rhododendron bushes, Purdey poked her head up a fraction of an inch, took her bearings and headed straight for the open gateway.

Gambit stopped firing, letting the Sterling dangle limply from his shoulder as he grasped the sides of the car and hung on for grim death. The Lancia shot out through the gates at over fifty mph, immediately screaming into a suspension-shattering, tyre-peeling right turn. Purdey continued down the road for several hundred yards before attempting to slow down.

Gambit threw himself into the passenger seat of the open car, whistling through his teeth. 'Nice driving,' he muttered, settling down into the seat and tossing the Sterling over his shoulder into the back of the car.

Purdey smiled. 'Nice shooting,' she responded. 'Hit anything?'

Gambit grinned. 'Took the heads clean off a couple of sunflowers,' he told her. 'And the garden gnome by the lily pond took it full in the gut.'

Purdey faked a shudder. 'Nasty,' she murmured. She stamped down hard on the accelerator. The powerful engine responded beautifully, the sleek Lancia surging forward as if fired with a sudden greed to devour the road itself.

Gambit strained his eyes into the cloudy sky.

'See it?' Purdey yelled, above the roar of the engine.

Gambit shook his head. 'Not yet,' he told her. 'Just keep going as fast as you can. There's no turning off this road for at least four miles.'

'Right,' Purdey shot back. As she spoke, she wrenched on the steering wheel. The Lancia shot across the road, mounted the opposite kerb and left the ground, clearing a narrow ditch and carving a huge hole in one of England's green and pleasant hedgerows.

Gambit threw up his hands in horror as the front wheels of the Lancia thudded down into the soft earth of a ploughed field. 'What are you doing, for Heaven's sakes?' he screamed at Purdey.

She spoke out of the corner of her mouth, her eyes firmly glued to the rough passage ahead. 'Taking a short cut,' she told him. 'Like you said – there's no turn-off for four miles . . . so who needs roads? It twists and winds so much we can probably make up a good half-mile like this.'

The Lancia roared past a herd of grazing cows in an adjoining field, starting up a full-scale stampede which would have put John Wayne to shame. Gambit's attention was distracted for several seconds as he watched them. When he turned his eyes to the front again, he fervently wished that he hadn't. The nose of the Lancia was headed straight for a particularly sturdy-looking species of five-bar gate.

'Hold on to your hat,' Purdey screamed, slamming the car down into second gear and sending the rev-counter hammering against the metal stop at the end of the redline section.

The gate left its hinges with only a token squeal of protest, flying into the air and crashing, in pieces to the ground again.

Gambit opened his eyes again, blinking a couple of times in disbelief. 'We got through?'

'Solid, these old Lancias,' Purdey yelled at him. 'Built to last, they were.'

'Not at this rate,' Gambit said, going rigid again as Purdey swung the car round to avoid a couple of sheep. The rear wheels spun out on the grassy surface, sending the Lancia into a sliding skid. Turning into it to regain control, Purdey made the Lancia's chassis wobble like a jelly on springs. The old car threatened to shake itself apart before it finally straightened out.

'There,' Purdey screamed out, taking one hand off the wheel to point into the sky.

Gambit's hand snaked out, grasping Purdey's wrist and thrusting her hand firmly back on to the wheel. 'You drive – I'll look out for the helicopter,' he told her firmly. He fixed his eyes on the faint speck in the distance, checking its direction. 'It's heading north,' he yelled. 'Steed must have turned on to the old Mowbray road.'

Purdey nodded, swinging the Lancia back towards the road. At high speed, she drove parallel to the hedge, waiting for a suitable gap to present itself. A few hundred yards ahead, she spotted an open gate.

The Lancia swung out in a wide circle, wheels spinning against the grass. Straightening up again, Purdey aimed the bonnet towards the gap and took the car through as straight as a bullet, throwing the steering wheel round as the front wheels touched tarmac again. On two wheels, the car performed an impossible turn, speed-wobbled for a hundred yards and finally ran smoothly again.

Gambit pulled himself up in his seat, sucking in a deep breath and exhaling it quickly. Now that the crazy bucking of the car had stopped, he only wished that his stomach would follow suit. He was not used to feeling seasick in a car.

In top gear, and on a normal surface, the roar of the powerful engine died to a healthy purr. Gambit glanced over at the speedometer needle, wavering gently around the 85 mark. Glancing up into the sky, he was relieved to note that the helicopter was a much bigger blob in the sky. It was less than two miles ahead of them, he estimated.

'It's swinging west now,' he said to Purdey. 'Turn off left at the next crossroads.'

She nodded. Several seconds passed.

Gambit's voice rose in a sudden scream. 'Only slow down first!' He closed his eyes again as the crossroads loomed up and Purdey swung the wheel. The car screamed round the signpost in the middle of the road on the wrong side, narrowly missing the front fender of a Mini and leaving black trails of shredded rubber to mark its passing.

'You didn't tell me the crossroads were quite so near,' Purdey complained.

Gambit opened his eyes again. 'Crossroads? What crossroads?'

Purdey ignored him, slowing to a mere 75 to negotiate the double S-bend which had just been sign-posted. She just made it.

Gambit collapsed, resigning himself to a head of grey hair and a nervous breakdown. He lay back, his head on the top of the seat and his eyes glued to the helicopter. He wanted to see no more of Purdey's driving.

The hours, and miles, flew away. The helicopter headed steadily west. Gambit glanced down at his watch as the Lancia crossed over the border and entered Wales. They had been in pursuit of the helicopter for over three hours.

As the morning had passed, the sky had become increasingly heavy and overcast. Strong westerly winds were bringing in thick, ominous storm-clouds, heavy and swollen with rain. Several times, Gambit had feared losing the helicopter as the cloudbase sank lower and lower, prior to precipitation.

Now, as they roared through the tiny village of Coedpoeth, the clouds could contain their watery cargoes no longer. The rain fell in a heavy, swirling grey sheet, quickly turning the narrow road into a shallow river.

The sky darkened. Gambit, peering up and vainly trying to shield his eyes against the blinding rain, cursed under his breath as the helicopter winked out of view. 'Damn, we've lost it,' he cursed out loud.

Purdey concentrated on staring ahead. The windscreen wipers were doing their best to cope with the downpour, but it was certainly no clear view for the speed she needed to keep up. The rain poured into the open car, soaking both occupants to their skins, but there was no time to stop and put up the soft top.

A slightly darker speck showed itself against the black sky for a few seconds. 'There she is,' Gambit yelled. 'It looks like it's going down.'

He peered intently at the vague blur of the helicopter as it swung around in a slow circle, gradually losing height. There was no doubt – it was going to land. Gambit watched it until it disappeared behind a group of tall elm trees.

'Take the first turning off to the right,' he instructed Purdey. The road they were on curved steadily away to the south-west, and would lead them well away from the area in which the helicopter had gone to ground.

A small lane loomed up on the right-hand side of the road. Purdey swung the wheel hard, swerving across the road and just missing the overgrown bank which flanked one side of the lane.

As they travelled down it, Gambit realized that it was little more than a rough cart-track, just wide enough to permit a tractor to get through to the surrounding fields. Looking to either side, Gambit noted a small cluster of agricultural buildings, suggesting that they were on a private access road to a large farm property. The fields all around were tall with wild grass, utterly devoid of grazing animals. The buildings seemed to be in a considerable state of disrepair, indicating that the land and properties were derelict, and had been for some years.

'Look.' Purdy clutched at Gambit's arm.

Dead ahead, the narrow roadway came to an end, a large and well-bolted metal gate blocking off further passage. There was a low stone wall on either side, dismissing any thoughts Purdey might have entertained about another autocross session. Parked a few feet in front of the gate was Steed's Rover. It was empty.

Purdey pulled the Lancia to a smooth halt behind it, standing up in the car to stare out over the top of the windscreen. Just under half a mile away, across three open fields, stood a shabby-looking farmhouse.

Gambit slipped the Sterling around his shoulder and vaulted over the side of the car. 'Come on, girl. We're going to have to hoof it.'

Purdey nodded, throwing open the door and jumping down into the muddy land beside him. Together, they broke into a run, vaulting the low wall like a pair of

Olympic hurdlers and jogging across the soggy fields in the direction of the farmhouse.

As they ran, the fluttering sound of the helicopter's engine started up again. Ahead of them, the craft slowly rose again from behind the trees and coasted in towards the farm.

Gambit increased his pace, aware that it would mean leaving Purdey behind. Every second was going to count now.

Inside the farmhouse, Steed also heard the distinctive sound of the approaching chopper, and he cursed himself for a fool. He had taken every precaution against being followed, making frequent detours and constantly checking his rear-view mirror. No road vehicle could have possibly kept up with him without Steed's knowledge. He had not even considered the possiblity of pursuit from the air. It had been a stupid oversight.

Perov had played it smart all through the long chase. Instructing his pilot to stay well out of visual and audible range, he had homed in purely on the transmitter. Now, when Steed had already led him directly to his quarry, he no longer had any qualms about showing himself. The 'copter sank low over the thatched roof of the farmhouse, gently settling down in the abandoned pig-pens at its rear.

Chuckling exultantly, Perov clicked a fresh magazine into his Luger and jumped down into the slimy mud. He walked, slowly, towards the farmhouse.

Steed peered out of a grimy window and saw him coming with a sinking heart. He had neglected to arm himself, and the derelict farmhouse offered scant protection against a trained assassin, dedicated to his task.

Perov halted, twenty or thirty yards from the side of the house and brought the Luger up at arm's length. Squinting along it, he calmly loosed off a whole clip, shattering every window he could see. Reloading the gun, he repeated the procedure with the side door and moved round to the front of the house.

Perov walked jauntily. He appeared to be enjoying himself. Blowing out the front windows with six shots from his third clip, he allowed the gun to dangle at his side and called to Steed. 'Steed . . . forgive the pyrotechnics.' He waved his free hand towards the shattered windows. 'You must forgive me, really. A little extrovert, I must admit . . . but I needed to show you that I mean business.'

Steed's voice came from a downstairs room. 'What do you want, Perov?'

Perov laughed derisively. 'Come now, Steed. We are both too familiar with the game to fall back on childish delaying tactics. You know exactly what I want. You should also know that I do not have unlimited patience. Send Professor Vasil out to me. Soon.'

'And if I don't?'

Perov identified the source of Steed's voice, brought up the Luger and squeezed three more shots into the window frame. 'As you will have noticed, I have a clear shot at every exit,' he pointed out. 'I also have an incendiary grenade, which I shall toss into the building if Vasil does not come out in the next sixty seconds. An unpleasant death, cremation, Steed.' Perov broke off to laugh. 'Believe me, I should know.'

He delved into his pocket, withdrawing the grenade and holding it up. 'Just in case you think I am bluffing,' he shouted. 'You should know that Nikolai Perov never bluffs.'

There was silence. Perov waited patiently, finally

glancing at his watch. 'You have less than twenty seconds to make up your mind, Steed. Your death will be utterly pointless.' He broke off, looking back at his watch and mentally counting off the seconds. When he spoke again, his voice had taken on a distinctly petulant edge. 'You really are a foolish man, Steed. Six seconds . . . five, four, three . . .'

Perov drew back his hand to hurl the grenade. Steed's voice barked out.

'All right, Perov. You win.'

Perov smiled with satisfaction. 'Good, Steed. I see you have some sense after all. Please send the professor out to me at once. We are going home.'

The faint sounds of a scuffle came from the farmhouse. Perov called again, a little puzzled. 'What's going on on, Steed?'

Steed's voice was a little breathless. 'Quite understandably, Professor Vasil is rather reluctant to greet you,' he called. 'However, I assure you, he is coming.'

The front door opened. Steed, his bowler perched on the side of his head, staggered through it, dragging the screaming Vasil by the scruff of his neck. The two men struggled for a few more moments before Steed's superior strength won the day. He pushed the whining professor out of the door to fall face-down in the mud. Steed slammed the door firmly, cutting off Vasil's chances of retreat.

Vasil picked himself slowly up out of the mud. His heavy black overcoat was drenched and soggy with water. He stood, nervously, wiping his face and ineffectually trying to scrape the thick mud from his heavy glasses. He peered towards Perov uncertainly.

'Come along, Professor,' Perov called to him in a cheery voice. 'Our friend Steed no longer wants your company. He has chosen discretion as the better part of valour . . . a wise decision, under the circumstances.'

Vasil trudged, wearily towards him, his shoulders drooping. He looked a completely broken and frightened man.

'That's far enough, Professor,' Perov barked suddenly. He brought up the Luger. 'Sorry about this but you have to realize that I cannot afford to take any chances. The incendiary grenade could not have guaranteed your death . . . and unfortunately only your death will reinstate me. Goodbye, Professor Vasil.'

He squeezed the trigger gently. Vasil's body slumped backwards into the air as the slug slammed into his chest. He fell on to his back and lay there unmoving.

Perov took a couple of steps towards the still body, lowering the Luger. He took careful aim, preparing to make sure that his job was done.

'Perov!' Gambit's voice screamed across the hundred yards which separated them.

Perov whirled to face the unexpected threat. Gambit, running full pelt towards him, fired off a short warning burst from the Sterling. Perov fired two shots back before ducking down and making a run towards the waiting helicopter. As he threw himself into the cockpit, the craft began to rise, wheeling away over the top of the farmhouse.

Gambit dropped to his knees and brought up the Sterling into firing position. He blasted away at the rear stabilizing propellor, hoping to bring the aircraft down before it gained too much height.

The helicopter rose above the level of the farmhouse roof, banking away to the north. Gambit emptied the rest of the magazine, cursing as the trigger went dead. The helicopter continued to gain height, but was starting to behave erratically.

Gambit stared at it as the craft slowly began to spin in the air. The tail came up, so that the cockpit faced directly down to the ground. The rate of spin increased, becoming a dizzy spiral. Totally out of control, the helicopter plunged back towards the ground, exploding into a ball of flame.

Purdey ran up behind Gambit, panting for breath. 'Were you in time?'

Gambit shook his head sadly. 'He shot Vasil,' he muttered glumly. 'I don't know about Steed.'

He clambered to his feet and loped across towards the prone form of Professor Vasil.

The corpse stirred, groaned . . . and sat up! Gambit ran to Vasil's side, stooping to help as he dragged himself, painfully, to his feet.

'Are you all right, Professor?'

Vasil grunted as he straightened up. Reaching up, he picked off his heavy mud-stained glasses and wiped his face with the back of his hand. Gambit, seeing his face for the first time, did a double-take. 'Steed!'

Steed grinned ruefully. 'Couldn't let the poor old Professor step out into the line of fire,' he muttered. 'Wouldn't have been sporting.'

He unbuttoned Vasil's heavy topcoat and drew out a thick metal fire guard which had been wrapped around his chest. There was a heavy dent in one side of it.

Gambit stared at it in astonishment. 'God, Steed, are you all right?'

Steed nodded, wincing with pain. 'A couple of bruised ribs, that's about all,' he confirmed.

Gambit nodded his head towards the dent in the fire guard. 'What if Perov had tried a head shot?'

Steed shook his head emphatically. 'Not his style,'

he said, confidently. 'Perov was one of the old school . . . mean and nasty. A body shot every time, so if you didn't kill, you maimed.'

Purdey had ploughed through the mud to join them, just in time to catch Steed's last words. 'You could have been wrong,' she pointed out.

Steed nodded in agreement, smiling. 'True,' he murmured, simply.

The trio turned slowly, to gaze at the charred wreck of the helicopter. It was still blazing furiously, despite the heavy rain. No-one could have survived the inferno.

It was Purdey who put their shared thought into words. 'So Perov got his cremation after all.'

They stared at the burning helicopter until the last flames fizzled out and black smoke rose thickly into the air. Only then did they turn away and trudge slowly back towards the farmhouse.